Writing Baseball

THE SOUTHERN ILLINOIS UNIVERSITY PRESS SERIES

Off-Season

Eliot Asinof

OFF-SEASON

Southern Illinois University Press

Carbondale and Edwardsville

Copyright © 2000 by the Board of Trustees,

Southern Illinois University

Printed in the United States of America

03 02 01 00   4 3 2 1

DESIGNED BY JAMES J. JOHNSON

Library of Congress Cataloging-in-Publication Data

Asinof, Eliot, 1919–
Off-season / Eliot Asinof.
p. cm. — (Writing baseball)
I. Title. II. Series.
PS3551.S54055 2000
813´.54—dc21   99-32220
ISBN 0-8093-2297-8   CIP

The paper used in this publication meets the minimum requirements of American
National Standard for Information Sciences—Permanence of Paper for Printed Library
Materials, ANSI Z39.48-1992. ⊚

Writing Baseball Series Editor: Richard Peterson

For my son, Martin

You've got to be careful if you don't know where you're going, because you might not get there.

If you come to a fork in the road, take it.

—LAWRENCE PETER "YOGI" BERRA

Acknowledgments

My thanks to Ron Power's brilliant study of Cairo, Illinois, in his book *Far From Home*. Then there was Frederick Durenmatt's famous play, *The Visit*. I received masterful tutoring about small-town politics from the mayor of a town in New England who insisted on anonymity. (Readers of *Off-Season* will understand why.) The faculty and students associated with the English department of The Hotchkiss School were valuable critics of my early efforts, as were Bill Littlefield, Jeff Kisseloff, Julian Koenig, Alexis Lalli, and my son, Martin. I am especially grateful for the bold and perceptive editing of Richard Peterson, English Department, Southern Illinois University.

Off-Season

Shimmering in the late afternoon sun, the white stretch limo cruised by the flow of pickup trucks like a yacht on a river of old scows. Drivers waved, beeped a staccato of greetings to the unseen face behind the tinted windows, for this had to be John Clyde Cagle Jr., known throughout the sporting world as "Black Jack," coming home to Gandee, Missouri, to celebrate the nationally televised opening of Black Jack Field.

In the spacious back seat, he stretched his powerful six-foot-four, 220-pound body, hands clasped behind the thick black hair that draped the back of his neck. On his thigh, the jeweled fingers of Judith Pagonis tapped to the beat of Tina Turner's "What's Love Got to Do with It?," her seductive body moving like one who had danced in limos all her life. Instant stirring in his loins amused him, and he remembered how he had left Gandee eight years ago, an eighteen-year-old virgin who would jerk himself off in bed hoping to forestall recurring nightmares. Now he shut his eyes to wallow in the sensuality of her perfume (special exotic stuff she had discovered in India). Her uninhibited sexuality dazzled him, and because she made no demands on him, all other aspects of his life seemed perfectly arranged. "I make magic happen," she would whisper in his ear, crystals dangling from the bedposts. What's more, Judith was the daughter of Theodore "Ted" Pagonis, billionaire shipping magnate, recent owner of the Los Angeles Dodgers and Jack's hundred-million-dollar contract, a neat parlay if there ever was one. His friend and old road roommate Corky (nee Thomas Jackson Corcoran) had declared Judith to be the consummation of the Six *B*s of good living: BaseBall, Big

Bucks, Banging Broads. Black Jack Cagle had won them all, for he was the greatest pitcher in modern baseball, shoo-in for a third Cy Young Award, twice National League Most Valuable Player.

She saw the smile teasing his lips and had to know why.

"What?" she asked.

"I was thinking, on a list of the Ten Happiest Men in the World, I'd be right up there."

"Oh, lists!" she sighed. There had been so many of them. *Forbes Magazine* had him richer than all but Michael Jordan. *Esquire* had the two of them as the Hottest Unmarried Couple in America. *Sports Illustrated* named him Athlete of the Year. "At Bryn Mawr, they voted me the Girl Most Likely."

"Most likely to what?" he asked.

"They couldn't decide." Judith laughed.

Typical of her, he thought: she could be obvious and unpredictable at the same time. With Judith, everything that happened came out of the moment. "Sudden Judith," Corky said of her.

Then, from the front seat beside the chauffeur, came the voice of Jack's money and management.

"You guys like sushi?"

Gordon Stanley shifted his overweight middle-aged body to drape his left arm over the seatback. Catching the sun, gold cuff links peeked out of his blue-gray sharkskin sleeve. Like one who kept a record of what he wore from day to day, he seemed never to repeat himself from his unlimited wardrobe. "Did they teach you about clothes at Harvard?" Jack once dared to tease him. "For those of us who can't throw a baseball 106 miles an hour, we rely on the power of image-making." This was the man who had turned an insecure eighteen-year-old minor-leaguer into the intimidating persona that brought him fame. When Jack hit the first batter he faced, then brushed back the second, Gordon had labeled him "Black Jack." The straight-arrow crew-cut all-American boy, his look patterned after his decorated war-hero father, grew his dyed ink-black hair to near shoulder length, flaring out from his cap like wings on a hawk. Nor was he to shave for two days prior to his turn on the mound, the beard darkened to add menace. He was taught to scowl as if he were suffering the stench of rotten eggs, staring at the catcher under the lowered peak of his cap like one scheming to commit mayhem. "Mean" was a more marketable image than "gentle," so under no circumstances was he ever to smile, not even in the dugout lest some TV camera catch a glimpse of it. Whatever effect this may or may not have had on hitters, TV announcers reveled in it. Indeed, Gordon wrote copy for them: "Look at that face, will you? Could you possibly picture him kissing a baby's butt?" Or "Black Jack was born biting the obstetrician's finger!" Nobody wanted to admit it, but everyone knew that the devil was the more powerful of the two deities. Gordon turned Jack into a satanic figure. No interviews. He never spoke to reporters in the locker room. Gossip columnists were fed provocative anecdotes about him kicking barking dogs in the street or threatening obstreperous children who dared to ask him for an autograph, or telling off policemen who dared to stop him for going through a stop sign. His appetite for food and drink and party girls was exaggerated to make him into a Ruthian figure of unlimited capacities. He was trained to ignore everything and deny nothing. On the mound, meanwhile, he became the best and kept getting better.

"Oh, it's a sexy image, all right," Judith had agreed. There was nothing so erotic as a competent villain, especially in custom-tailored spandex baseball pants that hugged his muscular thighs and buttocks. Whatever this extraordinary violation of his nature, Jack was too shy to object—an irony he quickly learned to live with—especially since he didn't really know who he was anyway.

And now, a trip to Japan.

"We're looking at what could be three, four million for a two-week tour. Pitch a few innings of an exhibition game, a couple of talk shows, have a catch with the emperor."

"Sounds fine," Jack said.

"There's another two mill if we put your name on a Jap glove."

Jack tried to make a joke of it. "Just two?"

"Well, it's a definite maybe."

Just a question of numbers, Jack knew. Year after year, Gordon had sent the dollars spiraling like exploding skyrockets. He made all manner of things happen—like this trip to Gandee. Gordon's idea from the beginning. Donate two million to build a ballpark for his hometown with a special facility for Little League. A contribution to small-town America via the national pastime. (Even the Mean Man had a soft spot.) It would culminate in this trip, heroic hometown boy returns to national TV coverage. The best public relations imaginable worth untold millions more in good will. "As good as it gets!" Gordon had put it. Jack had nodded, accepting the proposal over a year ago and promptly forgetting about it. He always did what Gordon asked, and the money kept rolling in.

"You are my main man," a grateful Jack once said to him.

"You can thank Curt Flood."

"Who's Curt Flood?"

Gordon had jumped all over him. "My God, you're like the black ballplayers who never heard of Jackie Robinson. Flood sacrificed his career to fight the reserve clause that kept you dumb ballplayers in virtual bondage. He led the way to free agency so guys like me could make guys like you rich."

"Okay, thank you, Curt Flood," Jack had said.

"And Marvin Miller."

"Who's Marvin Miller?" Jack had asked, but even as he did, he remembered. Miller had organized the players union.

"Japan is lovely in the fall," said Judith in tones that promised sex in a field of lotus blossoms.

Jack suspected she'd been everywhere in the world. And now even Gandee, which was not his idea at all. They were supposed to have met in New York three days hence, but there she had been at the Los Angeles airport. She wanted to go slumming, he guessed, an adventure to talk about at Beverly Hills cocktail parties. He remembered the other side of the coin when she'd taken him to the opera. She loved Carmen, the sexy lady who drove men wild enough to kill her. Jack was in evening clothes for the first time in his life in the company of elegance that took his breath away.

Now, in this limo, she moved close to him, her magic perfume dazzling his senses as her hand settled firmly on this thigh. With Judith, sex was best as an improvisation, the more spontaneous the better. (Tina was belting out the chorus to "What's Love Got to Do with It?") It was the sort of stuff that turned his lust into a blessing. He had never known what it was to really love someone, not even his parents. This was better, or so it seemed. No pain, all gain. "Limo sex," Judith would say: "You come as you go." He had to laugh at the mystery of what she was about to do. He looked up at her smiling blue eyes, caressed her ivory skin and long blond hair. Sensing his desire, she circled his Adam's apple with her mouth, working her tongue over it. His head went back to give her better access while her nails teased flesh under his shirt. In time, her touch had him gasping, fingers curling around him snakelike creating a need so powerful, nothing else in the world mattered.

When it was over, they did not kiss. She simply backed off with a self-satisfied smile. Kissing was strictly for foreplay. Love was the insidious *L* word, never mentioned. Rich girl's sex, he thought, not like star-fucking groupies who wanted him to autograph their panties. "Hey, I'm a sexy angel!" she would say, then laugh at such an implausible thing.

"Look!" she cried out. "'Welcome to Gandee. Pop 6181. Home of Black Jack Field.'"

Her voice bubbled as joyously as a child's on Christmas morning, but what he saw turned pleasure into a mouthful of sawdust. Three black crows were perched on that sign, splattering bird shit over his name as they waited to get at a dead dog on the road. In that instant, he was cursed by a sickening memory a dozen years old. He was on his bike and saw crows feeding on a run-over dog in front of his house. It was Boone, a setter he loved, and he went wild, yelling and screaming to scatter them. Later, he saw bird shit on his baseball cap and he never saw a crow again without tasting a residue of bile.

He'd never believed in omens or superstitions or even the need for luck, but the sight of that sign left his stomach roiling at the first flush of fear. The limo had driven by, but the impact lingered like the stench of a skunk. He knew what it meant, all right. He had felt uneasy from the moment they'd arrived at the St. Louis airport.

"Isn't this exciting!" Judith persisted as if she had to justify her insistence on coming with them.

"Hey, you'll love Gandee," he said, putting his best face on it. "Nice, neighborly folks. Like when you drive on rainy days, you don't splash anyone on the curb, you just don't," teasing her with this, having ridden in her Porsche enough to note her skill at "wave-making," as she called it, splattering people ten feet away.

As the limo headed toward town, he saw ghosts hovering over everything but he spoke only of angels. There was the Pringle wire factory, an old brick building now boarded up. He'd had his first job there, pushing a thirty-six-inch broom one summer so he could play ball on the factory team, but he didn't mention the sadistic foreman who'd made him scrub toilets until the acrid stench of disinfectants permeated everything he wore. And when they passed the Burger King, he bragged about all the cokes and fries he'd eaten with friends, and the fun of pranks and food fights that made his teenage life seem like a TV sitcom, but he definitely did not mention Betty Anne Simms, the cashier who'd exploited his endless infatuation with her until he reeked of humiliation. When they passed the Motel on the Hill, he described his young fantasies of romantic episodes in velvet-draped bedrooms with king-sized beds and giant color TV screens but said nothing about

getting caught as a peeping Tom outside a window, for which he was
soundly thrashed by his father. In fact, he never spoke of his father to
Judith (or anyone else, for that matter) except in awe of his silver-starred
Vietnam War heroics.

"Your father, I can't wait to meet him!" Judith said. "My father
never goes to war, he just buys and sells the equipment."

Jack enjoyed the comparison, pleased at what his father meant to
others. He'd grown up under the shadow of a man who demanded too
much. Jack could never be good enough to command his respect—
a kid who stammered a lot, who occasionally wet his bed long past his
infant years. Now that he was coming home again, above all else, above
the hoopla of his two-million-dollar ball field and whatever else Gordon had dreamed up, he wanted his father's respect. He wanted to see
it in his eyes, hear words that came from the heart. He could ignore
the rest of whatever lay lurking under all the old Gandee garbage.
The opening of Black Jack Field would be the perfect occasion. Whatever this trip meant to Gordon and his bottom-line mind, to Jack,
nothing meant more than throwing out the first ball to his father on
national TV.

"He's one tough hombre," Jack said. "Like the way he eats an apple.
Stem, core, seeds, the whole goddam apple. Wait till you see him, still
a soldier, by Jesus. Not a phony bone in his body. Always neat as a pin,
crew cut and all. When he walks into a room you think, 'Stand up and
salute!'"

"They don't make 'em like that anymore," said Gordon.

"The lieutenant my father saved in 'Nam, he came to the house
with his family on the tenth anniversary, all the way from Oregon, just
to introduce them. He was a schoolteacher and every March 22nd he
would tell his class the story of what my father had done. The two kids
gave Dad a gold watch and hugged him around the waist. Oh, man,
when I saw that, I was proud!" Then he thought how he'd felt, that he
could never be the man his father was, but he didn't say that.

Came then the sudden demands of Judith's bladder.

"Gotta go!" she let it be known, pointing to the towering "Shell"
sign a half mile ahead. Gordon signaled to the chauffeur to pull over.
"Might as well refuel." The chauffeur nodded and moved into the
right lane.

Jack gasped at the sight of the Shell station, his heart pounding
with resistance. No, not there. He didn't want to stop there. Words of
protest locked in his throat as the limo pulled up to the pumps.

"Come pee with me, Jack," she said, squeezing his hand.

He didn't need that either.

"Hey, this is Gandee, baby," he said.

"What can happen? Your daddy is sheriff!"

He pushed open the limo door for her. "It's to the left," he said. Then he watched her perfect body in motion, but even that could not stay his uneasiness.

Jesus, the Shell station! He had to wonder at the weird forces working to screw up his head, leaving him trapped where he definitely did not want to be. It had no right to happen this way, as if her bladder were part of a wily conspiracy to mess with his head. Had that fifty-foot sign sent a charge through her urinary tract? Was it there in the cards, right from the beginning, from that day Gordon first mentioned his idea for this project over a year ago? Jack could have stopped it then. He had wanted to stop it. He just couldn't come up with a reason. Nothing came to mind that could override Gordon's enthusiasm. He simply let it ride, then forgot about it. What the hell did it amount to anyway?

"C'mon, I'll buy you a coke," Gordon said, fumbling in his wallet for small bills. "You got change of a fiver?"

Immediately Jack shook him off without even checking. The mere mention of five dollars was still another jab at his memories.

Jack simply stayed in his seat, arms folded across his chest, his legs stretched out across the jump seat, his eyes shut like one about to take a nap. But he couldn't shut out the smell. It was the smell that hit him the hardest. When the fragrance of Judith's perfume gave way to oily rags and pumping gas, Jack was beaten by a memory slithering around inside him like an army of snakes. He was a sixteen-year-old kid on a day with a load of losses, pushing his broken bike from Burger King, where he had suffered still another rejection from Betty Anne. Inside this same garage a fat black kid was fixing a tire, so befouled in greasy sweat he seemed to have reached the outer limits of filth. Jack caught the body stench even as he entered. "Fat nigger sweat," his father would call it. "A fat man is an insult to God," his father would say. Jack had then seen one whose body seemed a creation of the devil, a black snowman with a blubber face made all the more sinister by a hideous scar across his right cheek. Beside him, a boom box belted out black man's rap in nasty sounds that threatened to drive Jack up the wall. It was maybe the first time in his life Jack was in full agreement with his father.

"Hey, can you fix my wheel?" he called out.

The response was complete indifference like one who was not only ugly but deaf. Jack reached for the boom box button and cut off the blare.

"Hey, my bike is busted!" he said.

The other kept working on the tire, two gnarled fingers on the left hand adding to the grotesque sight until, finally, without looking up, a soft mocking voice came back at him.

"Man, you pissed off all the time?"

"What's that supposed to mean?"

"I seen you pitch, that's what." And he shook his head in total dismay. "Hooo-eee! You might as well be throwing rocks at mad dogs."

Jack felt the back of his neck bristling, rage bubbling in his throat. "My bike."

"Pitchin' ain't no street fight, it's art, man. You gotta love it, like playin' a geetar to a beautiful chick. All that smoke you got is blowin' away!" Then, the kicker: "Ain't nobody ever showed you how to pitch?"

It was the "you-gotta-love-it" that scalded him, a phrase that summed up the story of his sixteen-year-old life. What he had loved the most had become the source of his unhappiness. His father had taught him how to catch, throw, and hit but constantly demeaned his talents, immersing the boy in a prophesy of failure. Then, one spring afternoon the stringy ten-year-old had hit a towering shot over the Little League fence, which no one had ever done, and young Jack circled the bases with a greater joy than he had ever known. In subsequent games, no one could get him out, Jack having found a God greater than his father. In the outfield, he ran like a deer and caught everything anywhere near him. Year after year, he proved his growing talents again and again until, one portentous afternoon, the fifteen-year-old threw a clothesline strike from deep center field to nail a runner trying to score. His father, then, found a new mission in their lives. "The pitcher is king," he said. "The game revolves around the man on the mound!" So the young outfielder was put on the mound where the cycle of failure began again. Jack hit batters with his powerful left arm and watched them crumble in tears. He walked far more than he fanned. He never conquered his nervousness, forever aware of his father's scorn. He was so wild, they called him "The Joker", a name he heard so many times that it fastened to his psyche. His catcher was totally unable to handle his speed. He would start games praying this would be the day he could hit the strike zone, but he always knew he couldn't. Two or three innings later, they'd put him back in the outfield. He had begun to hate the game of baseball, the only thing he had ever loved.

And always there was Betty Anne Simms to make it all the more painful. This first romance of his teens had become a horror story. She loved to tease him, jiggling her sexy little body to drive him crazy. He would get erections he couldn't control, embarrassing himself until he took to wearing jocks to conceal them. She would come to ball games, always with another boy, and sit behind the backstop where he couldn't help but see her. He would throw right at her, trying to drill it through the screen. Sometimes he thought she was the only target he could hit. His father, his wildness, his obsession with Betty Anne became the tripod of his misery.

("You gotta love it.")

Jack disliked everything about this kid in the garage. Combine the fat and filth with the smart-ass style and you couldn't disgust him more. He had grown up wary of all blacks. One way or another they bothered him. This one was about as bothersome as they came. He was making quick moves as he tinkered, little moves with his head and hands as if he didn't know how fat he was. His father used to warn him: "Niggers come in two kinds: them that don't give a goddam about nothing, and them that pretend they do." Jack stared at this one thinking, "Shit, he's probably both."

"Goddam it, fatman, can you fix my wheel?"

Finally, the other had acknowledged him, "Fix anything," he said, then turned the bike upside down to rest on the handle bars and spun the foot peddle as he watched the gear mechanism. In less than a few minutes, he found the dislocation in the gear line. In a few more minutes, he repaired it.

"Ten bucks, man," he said.

"What! For that?"

"I fixed it, man. You couldn't."

"I've only got five," Jack said, hating this.

"Gimme five, owe me five."

Jack gave him the five dollars and turned to leave. Straddling the seat, he paused, eager to turn this scene around.

"What makes you such an expert on pitching?" he asked.

"I'm a catcher."

Jack laughed at him. Not a high-jumper? Not a sprinter?

"Maybe you should use a mitt," Jack said, pointing to the distorted fingers of his left hand.

"I got a mitt. I'm lefty."

"What! I never saw a lefty catcher."

"There ain't too many. My granddaddy caught lefty. He caught Satchel."

Yeah?

"Who did *you* catch?" Jack teased him.

The other smiled, shaming him for the question by refusing to answer. He smiled at his little secret looking as if he had caught everyone from Satchel to Koufax. Jack was moved to ask, "Where you from? I never seen you before."

"Kansas City. Moved here a couple months ago."

"Catcher, eh. You got a mitt?"

"My granddaddy's."

Sure thing. A rotten old rag. Jesus, what a joke. If he threw hard to him he'd likely kill him.

"Bring it tomorrow. Okay?" he said. "Better bring a mask and all, just for protection."

"Five o'clock, Joker," he smiled. "And you bring the fiver you owe me."

"My name is Jack Cagle," he corrected him.

"Cyrus Coles," said the other.

Cyrus was sitting in the shadows, a young black girl beside him as slender as he was fat and as loving as Betty Anne was not.

"This's Ruby," Cyrus introduced them.

"Sheeeit, he ain't even got a glove!" said Ruby, sounding like a child crying out that the emperor had no clothes.

Jack paid her no mind. What's the big deal? He could throw without a glove, couldn't he? Hadn't he come to see if Cyrus could catch?

Cyrus was fondling a new baseball in the folds of a frayed black leather mitt with almost no padding around the cavernous pocket.

"There ain't nothin' like a new baseball. All them wound-up bands inside, the smooth hide sewn tight. Put fingers on them seams, you feel like you can throw it through a wall. You dig, man? Ain't it a perfect piece of work?"

"Let's see it," Jack said.

Cyrus shook his head. "You ain't no pitcher without a glove."

"Bullshit!"

Cyrus sighed, turning to Ruby. "Baby, you know why this white boy so badass? He made a wrong turn up Pussy Street!"

Their laughter left him seething. This fat filthy nigger had turned his love life into an obscenity! How did he know, anyway? That *he* should have a girl friend and not Jack was too much for him. He demanded the ball with his eyes, furious that nothing was going his way.

Ruby broke the silence, glaring at him with steel gray eyes.

"You a real piece of shit, man. You ask him to bring his mitt? He brings his mitt. He buys a new baseball with the five dollars. He takes me in back to help him measure off the slab and the home plate. He wants everything to be right because he is Cyrus Coles." She paused to let that penetrate. "Now s'pose you go fetch your glove and the five dollars you owe. Then maybe if y'all show some respect you'll have some for yerself!"

"Wooo-eee!" said Cyrus.

Well, to hell with this bullshit, Jack thought, then pulled away on his bike with no intention of returning. He would never know why he did. In his room, he put his glove on his right hand, punched the pocket, then quickly laid it back on the shelf. He went to the kitchen for a Coke, taking his time drinking it. He needed a victory to counter his frustration, especially over a fat nigger who thought he was hot shit.

When he came back with his glove twenty minutes later, they hadn't moved. He didn't have the five dollars and he had no intention of repaying it. He had come back to punish this kid for his arrogance with murderous fastballs.

Cyrus led him around the garage where he had set up a two-by-four slab for the pitcher and a plywood square for home plate. It had been several days since Jack last threw to his father, so he warmed up slowly. Cyrus threw the ball back with hard whip-like flicks of his wrist requiring no more energy than pulling a trigger. Then sensing Jack was ready, he squatted, centering the old black mitt in front of him.

Jack was ready, all right. Ready to all but kill him. His pitch was high, just over Cyrus's head, and the mitt snapped at it like a hungry snake at a jumping frog. And back it came, returning anger with admonition.

"Why you lookin' off, man? You ain't at Burger King. Look at the mitt! It's cock high, man. Look at the mitt!"

Fuming, Jack threw at his head again, and missed inside.

"Man, you lettin' go too quick. Bring it down to me. Bring it all the way down!"

It took five or six more throws before Jack realized what was happening: he wasn't testing or intimidating Cyrus, Cyrus was trying to teach *him* something. Besides, he could have thrown a thousand pitches, Cyrus would have snapped them back as fast as he grabbed them. Fat as he was, he had the quickest mitt Jack had ever seen.

"C'mon, c'mon! Eyes on the mitt! There ain't nothin' in your life but the mitt!"

For all his rage, Jack stared at it. Even before he began his next motion, he fastened on the sight of it. Slowing his tempo, he brought the ball down and hit the target for the first time. Then he hit it again, and again, and began to throw harder. Suddenly, it seemed as if that mitt was blessed with a magnetic power. He hit it repeatedly. Six, seven, eight times. This never happened when he threw to his father.

"Lift your leg, man! Take the arm back further, yeah, and keep them eyes on the mitt!"

Harder and harder, the more he hit the mitt, the harder he threw, making sharp popping sounds he never heard before. Cyrus began moving the target off center. Inside, outside, low, high, it didn't matter where. Jack never took his eyes off it. Then Cyrus called Ruby to stand at the plate like a batter, an old broom stick to simulate a bat. It was like William Tell setting an apple on his son's head. Jack hesitated, afraid he might hit her. But Cyrus kept on him. "Don't look at no hitter. You don't see no goddam hitter. Just the mitt. It's suckin' you in. It's the momma and you the daddy. It's the pussy, man. Bring it into the hole!"

And so it happened. When Cyrus moved Ruby to the other side of the plate nothing else changed. Jack fought back laughter as he threw strikes because this was definitely the most beautiful goddam thing he had experienced since that first Little League home run.

When Cyrus decided it was enough, he tucked his mitt under his arm and kissed Ruby.

"Baby, you just seen the best!" he said.

She laughed. "I didn't see nothin'!"

"That's what I mean!" said Cyrus.

Time and again, throughout the summer, Jack came back to that Shell station. From Cyrus, there was something new every time, some minuscule adjustment that added power and stability to his delivery. All unnecessary movements were eliminated. He could throw a hundred pitches and not feel tired. He could feel that old black mitt sucking him in. He could see it in his dreams. He began to see himself as a pitcher.

He never told anyone, least of all his father. When he threw to his father, he was deliberately wild, using his new skills to imitate old failures. Once, when his father happened to drive by the Shell station and saw him biking away, Jack was ready with an explanation. He had even rehearsed it. "Had to get air in the back tire." There was no fat nigger catcher with an old mitt that had once caught Satchel Paige, no leather pussy with magical power, no slab behind the garage. None of this had happened. Besides, this wasn't even a ball field much less a game. He was like a soldier firing at bullseyes on a rifle range where no one was shooting at him. In town games he played during that summer, he stayed in the outfield for which everyone was grateful. Everything would wait for the following spring.

Cyrus Coles became his high school battery mate out of default. It was enough that no one else could catch his speed. And when Jack began to throw strikes, everyone believed it was part of some inevitable development, a coming of age that blessed all talented young athletes. In that one season, the seventeen-year-old John Clyde Cagle Jr. became invincible. Cyrus, who could neither run nor hit, was never thought to be a factor. It seemed simpler and even appropriate that Jack never suggested otherwise. After all, he had always been one helluva ballplayer, just as his father had been. Having grown four inches and added fifteen pounds since the previous season, it was easier for him to believe what everyone believed, especially since his father put a genetic spin on his first shutout. When there was another shutout, Gandeeans agreed: "Like father, like son," they said. They even had the same names, didn't they?

Throughout that triumphant season, Cyrus kept him disciplined, no hollering necessary. The squat body and the centered mitt were enough. Having learned to pitch over the previous summer, Jack could feel the difference in his stride, his kick, his release. It seemed to him that his timing came out of his body fluids. His concentration was unfailingly intense. Betty Anne could have danced naked on the dugout roof and he wouldn't have noticed.

Then came the big league scouts, all the way to Gandee from Chicago, St. Louis, and even Los Angeles, seduced by the big young lefthander's ninety-mile-an-hour fastball and string of shutouts. The scouts came repeatedly through the season and were never disappointed. They were all there at the Southeast Missouri Regional playoff game in June to see the undefeated kid with the poise of a veteran, smoking strikes by hitters, rarely more than a dozen throws an inning. In this state of grace, he could have gone on pitching forever. At the end of eight innings, Jack returned to the bench leading 1-0 when suddenly, there was his father sitting where no parent had a right to be. Jack winced at the sight of that gleaming Sam Browne belt, thinking Good God what have I done! It was eight innings of a *perfect game* as it turned out. He hadn't realized it. Not one man had reached first base. For the first time, he hadn't walked anyone! "This is your big moment, Son! Don't blow it!" came the arrogant demand, leaving him to stew in one last challenge to his seventeen-year-old equanimity.

Jack sat alone on the end of the bench, suddenly nursing a buzzing in his ears. He felt an enormous thirst but was barely able to swallow. It was as if someone had delivered a death threat that clung to his sweating body. He should have said something but no one would talk to him. Not Cyrus who was in the on-deck circle waiting to pop-out, or the coach (his chemistry teacher) at third base. To have a no-hitter going was supposed to be unmentionable. To speak of a perfect game had to be a capital crime.

When he returned to the mound for the start of the ninth inning, his stomach rebelled at the terror coursing through him. When he faced the first hitter, he pleaded for a thunder storm to rescue him. He stared at Cyrus's mitt, unable to find focus. He stepped off the mound, went to the resin bag mumbling idiot words of encouragement. When he threw his first pitch, it soared over Cyrus's mitt, into the screen fifty feet behind the plate. It was so wild, he stood on the mound grinning. His second pitch was in the dirt, and he heard the nervous crowd sounds. He could see the visitors' dugout coming alive, bats banging on the dugout steps. He worked fast, thinking all he needed was one strike to turn it back. His third pitch was outside, signaling the coming end of the perfect game.

He tried to rally his composure, thinking, okay, he'd walk this guy. What was so terrible about just a no-hitter? He began to landscape the mound with his spikes but there was no relief from the butterflies fluttering in his gut. He heard that old cry "Joker!" from the visitors' dugout, a dozen kids yelling at him. In the stands, the crowd was on its feet, screaming at him. "Do it! Do it!" Anything less would be a defeat. Well, tough shit, he thought. It ain't gonna happen, not this time.

Then, suddenly, he saw Cyrus rise from his squat and walk slowly to the mound. Jack scowled at him. He didn't want to hear any more bullshit. Anything and everything was futile; he was going to walk this guy and get on with the no-hitter. He stood tall on the mound, waiting, daring Cyrus to defy his mind-set.

They were words he never expected, never repeated, and never forgot:

"You dead-beat honkey mother-fucker, I just remembered: *you still owe me five bucks!*"

And to punctuate the charge, he tapped Jack in the gonads with the mitt, then turned back to the plate.

Jack was stunned. It was so crazy, he couldn't absorb it, so out-of-whack with the terror pumping through his body, it knocked the breath out of him. Cyrus's words simmered until the laugh-bomb exploded in his brain. He felt himself give way to its power and turned his back to conceal the impact. To be capable of laughter at that moment was akin to a miracle. His eyes began to tear and he turned toward the outfield, shielding his face with his sleeve like one wiping away sweat. "Up yours, Cyrus," he mumbled as he went for the resin bag, shaking his head at the enormity of his relief. When he finally went back to the rubber, he spun the ball lovingly in his hand, his fingers alive on the seams. He looked at Cyrus for his sign and saw five fingers splayed out in his crotch, not a sign but an appendage to his joke. Jack smiled, then shook him off. There was no need for signs now. He had but to drill it in. Once, twice, three times and the lead-off man retreated to the dugout, shaking his head. Jack got the second hitter on a one-hopper back to the mound. With two strikes on the third, he popped him up a few yards behind the plate. Cyrus circled under it but the ball hit the heel of his mitt and fell to the sod. As the crowd screamed in fury, Cyrus picked it up, tossed it back to the mound, then calmly returned to the plate. Two pitches later, Jack threw a blazing third strike across the knees, the umpire punched him "Out," and the great game ended the way it ought to end. By dropping the pop foul, Cyrus had made certain of it.

Teammates mobbed him as the crowd poured onto the field, bodies tumbling over each other in a jubilant melee. Cyrus, never one to join such celebrations, disappeared. When Jack finally got back to the locker room, he found the game ball in his shoe.

Two days after the major league draft, in front of TV cameras came the inevitable announcement of a major league contract with the Los Angeles Dodgers as Jack handed that game ball to his father, "The Man Behind the Gun" they said of him, a neat turn of phrase that referred to the decorated war hero as well as Jack's early-on baseball coach.

In the whirlwind days that followed, there was no mention of Cyrus. They flew Jack to L.A. for the signing itself with its five-hundred-thousand-dollar bonus, a night at Chavez Ravine and his first meeting with big leaguers, a day at Disneyland, then on to the Dodger's farm club in Yakima, Washington. He never saw Cyrus. He was swept away before he had a chance to consider it. And when he stood on the mound again, he faced a professional catcher. There was no more Gandee, no more Cyrus. All signs pointed to the biggies. In such an ideal new world, he had no past, no room for memories.

He had never come home again until this day, a history that took him from that busted bike to the sleek stretch limo, from a wrong turn up Pussy Street to the beautiful blond daughter of his billionaire club owner. From the teenager Joker to Black Jack Cagle, the world's greatest pitcher.

He had come full circle with his memories, but he couldn't walk a dozen yards to where it all had happened—back there, behind the garage, where he had pitched to Ruby with her broomstick for a bat. He couldn't get over having done that. Cyrus had taken him beyond his reach, transformed his growing body into a marvelous machine. Cyrus had had the power to re-create him. Cyrus had made magic happen as if it were a religious experience. Cyrus had changed his life but Jack had pretended otherwise because that had been the convenient thing to do. Even then, they had never spoken except on the ball field, or in the dugout. They were battery mates, nothing more.

He didn't want to go back there. When no one knows, no one cares. You have but to conceal it from yourself and all will then be right with your world.

He could have gone back. He could have scruffed around in all those weeds to see if the two-by-four slab was still there. Its absence would be a fitting end to his memory. He would like that, the whole Cyrus story dissolving in a long-gone, rotted away two-by-four.

But he didn't go, preferring the pretense that it didn't matter. The truth was, he was afraid that if he did, he might find it. He'd have to set his left foot on it again, face the force of his memory across 60 feet 6 inches of weeds after those eight years pretending that it hadn't really happened.

But it had. Just being here was enough to shake him up. He thought of calling Corky, making jokes about crow shit on the "Welcome to Gandee" sign, limo sex with Judith. He would not mention the Shell station, for he had never once spoken of Cyrus. Corky, however, had a way of seeing through Jack's bullshit. He'd get Jack to say things he had no intention of talking about. It was as if Corky could see into his head.

Then there was Gordon again to rescue him.

"Why do I always hope that a shithouse won't smell like a shithouse? Can you smell Gandee, kid? I'll tell you something: you could drop me blindfolded in Worcester and I'd know where I was at the first whiff. Year after I graduated Harvard I stopped my BMW at a service station a lot like this, a guy comes out and says 'Hey, if it ain't ol' Stinky!' Goddam. Not long after that George Stanky became Gordon Stanley, and I don't go back to Worcester."

"I know what you mean," Jack said.

"You and me, we're a lot the same. We both got out. I had this preppy friend at Harvard, taught me how to play the money game. Wear the right clothes, use the right words. Say 'basically' every once in a while, or 'really?' Speak with the right tone of voice. Even the woman I married, she had to be the right sort of gal, not too smart and definitely not too good-lookin'. I didn't want my wife to seem threatening to other wives. Best thing I ever did was marry ol' Ellen. I take that woman to bed and I think, hey, because of her, everybody trusts me. She may be a dog but so what, it pays off in the daytime."

"Hard to think of you as 'Stinky,' Gordon."

"Self-made men, you and me. We make adjustments. That's always the secret kid. Adjustment."

Jack nodded, pleased with this kind of talk. The Harvard man had wiped off Stinky and Black Jack wiped off Cyrus. Everything was now neat and tidy. He liked Gordon. Not only made him super rich, he made him feel good.

Judith returned with a bright red ribbon over her long blond hair, walking with her look-how-beautiful-I-am moves, smiling seductively as if this was what her life always came down to. When Corky first saw that look, he had a line for it: "She looks like somebody who never heard any bad news."

Gordon sighed, shaking his head in awe. "Kid, you are one lucky sonovabitch!"

She kissed Jack like a long-gone lover. "Remember me?" she whispered. "We met in a bordello in Istanbul."

"You were the best," he said.

Actually, they had met seven months ago in the children's ward of a Los Angeles public hospital. He was there on a media photo op at the bedsides of poor sick kids, autographing Black Jack baseball cards, cheering them up with assurances of a quick recovery whatever the ailment, and to prove it, he promised to strike out Ken Griffey Jr. that night. "Just for you, Billy," whereupon the TV cameras would lap it up as he ruffled the kid's hair, the tamed monster, the savage beast turned pussy cat for the moment. The real Black Jack would reappear on the mound. And there was Judith, a volunteer social worker in sedate tailored clothes orchestrating the action. One minute at this bedside, three minutes at another depending on which kids were appropriately photogenic—like little Billy with his bright eyes and wistful face. Ordinarily, he would have hit on a woman that beautiful, but her elegant style cut him down. She looked as if she could run the world. Her superior tones suggested you don't have to really care in order to please anyone, all you had to do was pretend that you do. Of course, he was aware that she was the club owner's daughter, which only made her all the more intimidating. She never so much as smiled at him. She carried her head high, and the quiet command of her voice exuded privilege. He found out later that she was a Bryn Mawr graduate doing her little do-good thing, much like himself. She would give the hospitals two afternoons a week—unless she had something better to do. She was Judith Pagonis and nothing more was expected of her.

As she got back into the limo, the chauffeur was running Windex spray and a squeegee across the windshield, vainly trying to remove splotches of dried bird shit. With a sudden fury that astonished them all, Jack bounded out of the limo, scooped up a handful of dirt and smeared it roughly over the surface with his bare hands.

"Good God, what's got into him?" Judith murmured.

"Whatever. Just don't ask!" said Gordon.

Jack used his handkerchief to wipe his hands, smiling sheepishly as he got back in the limo.

Then Gordon went back to work.

"There'll be an escort waiting for us in town. TV trucks, mucho cameras, the whole network bit. I want you to keep these windows rolled up. No pictures of you until you step out onto the field, Jack. Let them shoot the limo en route. Adds mystery and drama to the arrival. Okay?"

Jack reached for Judith's hand but she was busy with compact and mirror. He sat back, staring out the window as they moved by vaguely familiar sights. Everything seemed shabbier than he remembered, as if the years had blighted the town under a polluted cloud. He had grown up where pride demanded neatness whatever the size of one's income, where even poverty was no excuse for slovenliness. What he saw now depressed him, a violation of his father's standards. "Just like Rodeo Drive!" Judith joked. Seeing the decay through her eyes made it all the more distasteful.

Then they passed an old pickup truck with a pile of junk in the bed, and from the driver's window a bony black hand emerged, its middle finger raised to greet his passing. Jack grunted, stifling his need to take vengeance, unseen and unheard behind the tainted window, satisfying his troubled soul by mumbling "Up yours!" under his breath.

"Welcome to Gandee." He actually spoke the words.

In the center of the town square, the great bronze statue of Colonel Evan Gandee on horseback, the Indian fighter who had given the town its name, towered over fire trucks covered with red, white, and blue bunting. At the limo's approach, they greeted his arrival with a sound system blaring John Philip Sousa's "Stars and Stripes Forever." A truck away, a TV camera crew was mounted on a flat bed, ready to roll.

There were "Welcome Home Jack" signs everywhere, and the town was smothered by blaring sounds and bunting-covered windows.

Two miles down Carson Road, the motorcade reached Black Jack Field, where the sounds of Sousa gave way to the Gandee High School band playing "Take Me Out to the Ball Game." The stands were jam-packed with Black Jack baseball caps, three thousand plus, maybe half the population of the town. Others filled the area behind the foul lines.

Everyone rose to greet him, dancing in place as they waved black and white Black Jack Bar candy wrappers, so many in one congested area, the sweet smell of its licorice permeated the air.

"Well, all riiiight!" Gordon sang out, for he had, in fact, arranged for the free candy bars as well as baseball caps with the Black Jack sportswear logo. He had also orchestrated the grand entrance, directly to the mayor of Gandee himself, and there he was on the pitcher's mound in the center of it all.

"Uncle Sam!" Jack cried out, for Sam Manning was indeed Jack's uncle. A small wiry man with dark curly hair and amber-rimmed bifocals that rested high on the bony steeplechase nose of his ratlike profile. He always wore sport coats and slacks of garish colors. Tonight, the combination had to be the brightest in his wardrobe, a burgundy blazer with silver buttons over pastel peach slacks, and his necktie was a daring red-and-black striper. This was Mayor Sam Manning in all his glory.

Jack walked into Sam's open arms, a laugher for the long and short of it. The mayor made the greeting official by raising Jack's left arm as high as he could reach like a boxing referee declaring a new champion.

"They love me, kid," he grinned, the burgundy sleeve sweeping the area as if everyone was there because of him.

"You haven't changed a bit, Sam."

"Not bad for fifty-two, eh?"

And just as suddenly he was all strictly business. "Here's the program. Kids' teams come out, give you a baseball *they* signed. You thank them. Then I hand you the switch, and you push the button that turns on the field lights. You say a few words, you know, how happy you are about all this. Then you throw out the first ball."

"To my dad, right?"

Gordon had made that clear enough, for it was the best of all possible images. Here would be Sheriff John Clyde Cagle Sr. wearing his Silver Star, receiving the first pitch from his son. The man behind the sheriff's star was also the man behind the baseball star, the man who not only taught his son to be a great ballplayer but to be Black Jack tough about it. That was the way it came down to all sports fans.

Sam, however, had something else in mind.

"Yeah, but the *first* first ball you gotta throw is to your high school catcher—you remember, that fat colored boy."

"Cyrus Coles!" Jack blurted out the name before it could get caught in his throat.

"Him," Sam went on. "We had to get the colored into this, you know, with all the TV coverage. Good for racial amity."

Jack took the blow smiling like a fighter who refused to show weakness. He told himself there would be no problem. He had only to do what the mayor asked. He wondered if he had a five dollar bill in his wallet. Probably not. It had to be a fiver but there was no way he could fumble for it now. It even crossed his mind to tell the story of Cyrus at that perfect-game crisis, then hand Cyrus the fiver, his payoff at last for the world to see.

"Some of the colored here seem to think he made a big difference catching your stuff," Sam went on.

"Well, yeah. He did."

"Say that, kid. By all means, say that!"

Jack was stung, right on the heels of the Shell station memory, suddenly it was déjà vu all over again.

"Well, sure, sure. Whattaya know!" He worked for a smile to make light of his confusion. It had never crossed his mind that this might happen.

"You throw to him, kid. He comes to the mound. You autograph the ball for him and say a few words. The band starts up a drum roll and *then* your father comes to the plate."

Sam was reaching for the mike with a smile as nimble as his hands.

"Gandee is proud tonight," he began. "There are too many false heroes in this great country. Sometimes I think there's too much greed, too much selfishness among them. But not here. No, sir, not here. For we've got the great Black Jack, John Clyde Cagle Jr., Gandee's favorite son!"

There were rousing cheers.

"And now John Clyde Cagle Jr. has given back to Gandee!"

There were louder cheers, foot stomping, colors waving.

"Let me tell you, friends, America is watching us tonight. Gandee is no longer a dot on the map of Missouri, it's a town celebrating what is best about this great country! Because of this wonderful ball park, Gandee will be an inspiration to everyone!"

Jack felt the mayor's hand on his arm, his syrupy voice sounding as if it had been trained exclusively for this very moment.

"Who is the only pitcher in modern baseball to amass over three hundred strikeouts in four consecutive seasons?" he cried out.

"BLACK JACK!" the crowd roared.

"And who is the only pitcher who batted over .325 as pinch hitter on days he did not pitch?"

"BLACK JACK! BLACK JACK! BLACK JACK!"

"My friends, the name of the game is pride. And we take pride in what's happening here tonight. The greatest athlete in the whole world is standing here with us!"

The band took the cue and replayed "Take Me Out to the Ball Game," the crowd cheered, and two Little League teams in brightly colored uniforms marched to the foul lines. A team captain came with a baseball covered with autographs, momentarily paralyzed in the spot light as he stared at Jack as if he were in the presence of God Himself. Jack bent over to shake his hand as the mayor lowered the mike. The kid struggled for overly-rehearsed words: "We offer this autographed baseball to Black Jack Cagle in the hope that ten years from now, one of these names will be a major leaguer too!" Greeted by cheers, the kid handed Jack the ball, raised his hands high in a gesture of personal triumph, then ran from the mound to rejoin his teammates. Jack looked at the ball and read a few names. "Jake Hermans, Pete Storch, Tubby Troon. Hey, ten years from now, if one of you guys rips one of my fastballs out of the park, I'm coming back to tear this place down!"

Laughter. More cheers.

"Hey, everything the mayor has said is on the nose. This is a beautiful ball park. It makes me feel great to come back to Gandee, really great. It tames my savage Black Jack heart. It's the best idea I ever had!"

Cheers, rhythmic stamping of feet, a great unifying chant "BLACK JACK, BLACK JACK!"

Then Sam was beside him again, this time with the remote control switch.

"Let there be light, kid," he said.

A blast of trumpets was followed by a roll of drums to feed the drama. Jack held the gadget up for all to see, pushed the button and on came the overhead field lights, turning the grass to a glorious green. When one beam on the left field pole cracked, breaking glass, everyone cheered that too. Then the fife and drum segment of the band, six kids with a high-stepping majorette, came marching down the right field foul line toward home plate. The mayor handed Jack a new baseball, fresh out of the tissue-papered box. This would be the moment when Cyrus would walk onto the field with his granddaddy's catcher's mitt. Jack toed the rubber, twirled the new ball behind his back as was his style while waiting for the catcher's sign. He swallowed thickly, suddenly assaulted by a wash of sweat like one facing a serious crisis for which he was not prepared.

"He ain't here, Sam," a voice behind him was muttering. "He was supposed to meet me by the dugout."

"Goddam C.P.T.," Sam snapped back.

Colored People's Time, Jack knew. (His father would love to spit out those letters.) Jack sighed with relief, rescued from the brink of disaster. Cyrus, apparently, hadn't wanted the confrontation any more than Jack did.

Sam was ready, of course. The consummate politician was always ready, whatever the contingency.

"Friends, neighbors, Gandeeans, lend me your ears!"

Laughter.

"To receive the first pitch ever thrown on Black Jack Field, to be thrown by the great Black Jack himself, please welcome the man who made it all possible. Gandee's Silver Star Vietnam War hero, Sheriff John Clyde Cagle Sr.!"

Cheers.

Medals gleaming, the sheriff's uniform immaculately tailored on a trim never-changing muscular body, his black boots at high polish, the tan Stetson perched low over his forehead, from head to toe, here was the perfect image of an officer. It was often said he resembled John Wayne, but to him, John Wayne was a fake, all war movies were fakes, for John Wayne had never faced an enemy trying to kill him. Look at this man and you'd see the truth of it.

No Cyrus. Just the war hero.

Relieved beyond belief, Jack smiled at the difference. Everything about it was perfect. They would celebrate the father-son tradition that had bred baseball players for over a century. Gordon was right once again. How could it be any better than this?

John Clyde Cagle Sr. stood at the plate without so much as a gesture to acknowledge the cheers, not even a smile. He treated the moment as a solemn occasion, a let's-see-what-you've-got look as if the father would forever find a way to judge his son. Or so Jack read it, feeling the tug of old insecurities. Even his own wild bushy-haired Black Jack look seemed like a deliberate insult designed to provoke him.

As the drums began to roll, Jack toed the rubber, putting on his celebrated Black Jack game face. The crowd cheered, loving it, and he scowled, leaning in as if to pick up the catcher's sign, scowling again as he shook it off to feed this simulated drama. Then he spit, nodded, and began his windup. He threw leisurely for he hadn't warmed up, a typical looping toss as the drum roll accompanied its flight until his father caught it with his bare hand to the sound of the bass drum. A laugher of a climax, whereupon the sheriff walked to the mound showing neither pride nor amusement.

Their greeting, then, was not what Jack had hoped for. There was no embrace, just a formal handshake. TV cameras recorded the classic American father-son success story as the two walked off the field. Not Cyrus Coles but John Clyde Cagle Sr. The wrong man had become the right man.

And there was Judith to greet them, a gleaming beauty under the lights.

"Mr. Cagle, I must say, you're better looking than your son."

"Looks to me, that ain't sayin' much."

She laughed. "I never met a sheriff before."

"That so? We come in all sizes and shapes."

"You look just right to me, Mr. Cagle."

"Like they say ma'm, it's what's inside that counts."

Judith laughed. "Please, call me Judith." Then, daringly she kissed him on the cheek.

"Glad Emma didn't see that," he said. She was home, waiting for them. He explained that she'd felt a cold coming on.

"Well, then, let's go," Jack said.

"Mission accomplished," said Gordon.

Judith walked off, her hand under the sheriff's arm.

"I've never ridden in a sheriff's car," she said.

"Never rode in a limousine," he said.

Gordon, then, would follow in the limo.

They sat in the back behind the metal mesh screen, something new in Gandee.

"Like a New York taxi, Dad," Jack commented, hoping to start talking with his father.

But the sheriff ignored him.

They drove down Carson Road from the ball field toward Clark Street, the black section of Gandee. "Congotown," they called it. Then the sheriff turned onto West Road to skirt it, opting to go home on a country road.

"You sure threw me a blazer of a fast ball, Son." His sarcasm had the subtlety of a plane crash.

"Hey, Dad, I wasn't warmed up."

"On national TV, too."

Jack was going to apologize but thought better of it. Anything he might say could be used against him.

"It was good to see Sam, Dad."

"Your uncle is the heart and soul of Gandee."

"He's a pistol, all right."

"More like a cannon, Son."

"Okay," Jack sighed. "A cannon."

Judith stayed aloof from all this, staring out the window at the vast farm acreage in the pale light of a half moon.

"What's out there, Sheriff," she asked.

"Okra."

"In August, a thousand acres, nothing but okra," Jack said.

He reached for her hand picturing her with garden gloves snipping bougainvilla in her Beverly Hills garden. Today everything was loaded with contrasts.

They drove in silence as the police radio crackled with static turned low, more contrasts with the quadraphonic music in the limo, and then suddenly the radio came alive.

"John! John! Can you read me, John?"

In an instant, the sheriff turned up the volume. "What's up, Lem?"

"Homicide, couple hundred yards north of Lincoln Road, maybe a mile south of Clark Street."

The sheriff's voice sounded no more alarmed than if he was responding to a marooned pickup truck. "I'll be there in less than five, Lem."

He braked, backed up to reverse directions, set the party lights spinning and the siren wailing, and the tires spun rubber on the dirt surface as they passed the limo going away.

"Oh, my!" Judith cried out, not in horror but excitement.

"Sorry 'bout this," the sheriff said. "Duty calls."

"Oh no, don't be," she said. "I mean, it's great!"

"Like TV, eh."

"But this is *real!*" She squeezed Jack's hand, bubbling like a child.

A homicide! Jack had never so much as seen a dead body in his life, much less a murdered one.

In minutes, brightly colored lights were seen flashing above the fields. Another squad car, several pickup trucks, then a dozen or more people, all blacks. Lem Starger, the sheriff's black deputy, appeared in the headlights, keeping everyone away from a van tilted off the road shoulder. The sheriff stopped and got out in one quick move.

Then Jack, who had no intention of following him, saw the neatly printed logo on the side of the van: "Cyrus Coles, Plumbing and Heating." Within seconds, Jack was there to see Cyrus slumped over the steering wheel, blood covering his Gandee High School baseball shirt, blood splattered on the dashboard. Beside him, the old black catcher's mitt. Jack's heart pounded so vigorously, he couldn't catch his breath.

Minutes later, he realized that his dominant reaction was not horror but relief.

He could not avoid it. He was being spared for there would be no confrontation with Cyrus, ever. Anything that had happened behind that Shell station could now be wiped away. He let these thoughts seep through him, and though he tasted his guilt, his mind rallied with what he took to be his innocence. Some things were simply meant to be, or as Judith would have it, magic happens.

"Shotgun at close range," the deputy, Starger, was saying. "Looks like someone got in the van with him, made him drive off the road then popped him right here, maybe with his own gun."

"Sonuvagun!" the sheriff muttered. "Maybe it was light enough. Maybe someone saw. Somebody must've seen."

"Not out this way, John," Starger offered. "There's no one out here."

An ambulance pulled up, and two paramedics pushed through the crowd. A dozen or more cars had stopped, more people cluttering the area to the point of chaos.

"Dead maybe an hour or two," a paramedic said.

A police photographer was taking pictures. Close-ups of the wounds, the position of the body, the van. Jack was standing in the shadowy background when Sam spotted him, pulled him aside, laid an avuncular hand on his arm to keep him there. "This is bad shit, kid. Couldn't happen at a worse time, dammit."

"What do you make of it?" Jack asked, a pitiful question but he wanted to say something.

"Who knows? Who knows?"

"You mentioned race problems, Sam."

Sam nodded. Bad news began to spill out of his agile mouth like the staccato of muted machine gun fire.

"Cyrus was trouble, kid. Ask Lem. Had to lock him up a coupla months ago. Things are different here, kid. Big trouble on Clark Street. We got a nice little town with big city problems. Black on black, you know what I mean? Believe me, this ain't for you. The TV will be here any minute. With you around, it's big news, *bad* big news. Best you get out of here. Take your woman back to the house."

Sam left him to absorb the message but Jack kept staring at the van. Slowly, like one drawn by a powerful undertow, he made his way to it, wanting to see Cyrus one more time, to take a long close look, close enough to touch the body if he chose to, close enough to catch the stench of death. The body was as fat as ever, maybe more so. He felt an ever deepening sense of helplessness, and then for reasons he could not deal with, a quickening sense of fear.

Not C.P.T. but murder.

"Cyrus was big trouble, kid," Sam had said.

He wanted to leave, but first he had to talk with his father. His father would tell him everything he had to know. As Jack moved toward him, back to the van, he heard a shrill cry of agony, so strident it sent a chill through him. A small black woman was fighting her way to the van, defying the restraint of two men. It was Ruby Coles, and she kept on struggling until she collapsed in pathetic sobs. They sat her gently on the ground, out of sight of the bloodshed, and Jack recognized her brother Lukas, kneeling to comfort her. Then suddenly, as though she knew all along he was there, she was staring at him, tear-drenched, lips trembling. Struck by a force even greater than her grief, her face twisted into a look of such hatred, she seemed transformed. Her mouth tightened as her jaw locked tightly behind it. Whatever possessed her, Jack was not about to question it. Her torment demanded one last shot at him, and she mouthed "Fuck you, motherfucker!" with such venom he didn't have to hear to feel the force of it. It scalded him as if she were accusing him of the murder. What could he say to her? He avoided her eyes, afraid she would see through his gathering guilt. His best thought was to go back to the limo and get the hell out of here. But his feet felt as if he were stuck in concrete. Ruby had paralyzed him with her eyes.

He turned away, rallying to regain control. It was she who was the racist now. Not him. He wasn't about to suffer her scorn. It was all he needed to drive him off. Like Sam had said, Go! Get out of here! He had given the town two million bucks. He didn't need to suffer for his giving. Go, he told himself. Just go!

"So, they rained on your parade, eh Jack?"

Somehow he knew who it was, even before he turned to see her.

"Foxx," he said. The girl with two xs on the end and a first name no one seemed to know. "Yeah, Foxx," he repeated her name thinking she was the last person he might want to see here. "Long time, no see," he said. One cornball greeting deserved another.

She was just as he remembered her. Short red hair, freckled face, large horn-rimmed glasses over bright brown eyes. She was still wearing clothes like someone who couldn't care less what she looked like. Draped over her right shoulder was a woolen bag that seemed large enough to hold everything she might need for a month. She was a strange one, in no way typical of Gandee. He would have thought she'd have been long gone. At this confused moment, however, a part of him was pleased that she was there.

"So what's goin' on?" he wanted to know. If anyone knew, it would be Foxx.

She shrugged. On her freckled cheeks he saw the remnants of tears.

"Why don't you ask Ruby?" she replied, knowing that it had to be the last thing he would do. She was always the super smart one. President of the chess club. The debating team. She used her mind the way he used his left arm. Why wasn't she a lawyer in a big city? Or a professor at a college?

"You haven't changed much," he said, making conversation without caring one way or another.

"But *you* have, Jack!" There was no doubt of her disapproval. "You don't even look like you. That's not your face, it's a horror mask. I heard you on TV once after you'd hit a batter and sent him to the hospital. But you made a joke out of how the pitch just happened to get away because of a loose fingernail or something. 'I'm not a role model,' you boasted. What are you, Jack? Just another working stiff trying to make a living? Are you kidding? Why the meanness, Jack? What for? To sell shoes? Those commercials are so insulting. Why do you do them! For more money? I don't understand, isn't a hundred million dollars enough?" She kept going, all wound up, never stopping for a reply. It was as if she had waited years to dump this on him. "I remember that perfect game. You were so in love with what you were doing. The intensity was beautiful. Your shyness was endearing. It was you, Jack. But now it's all an act, isn't it. It's not for love anymore. That's so sad."

When she finally stopped, he jumped eagerly into the breach.

"So what are you doin' here anyway?" he asked

"I'm a reporter for the *Sentinel*. You remember the town weekly? It had a sports page, even comics."

She saw his look of incredulity. A reporter on the *Sentinel?*

"That's me," she admitted. "A little fish in a small pond."

A piranha, he thought.

"I don't do interviews, Foxx." Then, with a touch of the absurd: "Not even for the *Sentinel*."

"Actually, I had no intention of interviewing you. What could you possibly tell me I didn't already know? You say only what you're supposed to say. No siree, Jack, I came to the ball park to interview Cyrus Coles. Now *that* would be a story, don't you think? Fat black high school catcher comes to receive the first ball from his famous battery mate on national TV. Not a fast ball but a money ball. And you, Cyrus, how much money do *you* make? Can you imagine all the things that must have been going on in his head? And when you consider how it all came to pass, doesn't this have to be a really fascinating moment?"

It was as if she knew all about the Shell station. Had Cyrus told her? Or Ruby? Whatever, she could stick pins in him and make him squirm, like that moment in social studies class when the teacher had roused him from an afternoon daydream: "Jack, what can you tell us about the Nicaraguan Contras?" What? He didn't have a clue. He'd seen a few TV news shots of dead bodies that meant nothing to him. Not knowing what to say, he'd tossed out the first thought that came to him, a joke to fill the vacuum of his ignorance: "The Contras? What league are they in?" Everyone laughed, of course. Everyone except Foxx. "It's in the Death Squad League," she'd said. "The Squad that murders the most peasants wins. No umpires, no rules, the stats are the body counts. Just death, that's all there is, and the U.S.A. supplies the weapons!" In the biting silence of that classroom, Jack had felt like a clod of mud. Thank you, Foxx. Most of all, he remembered her voice with the same provocative edge, always on the brink of a joke that wouldn't be a joke at all.

He had never met anyone like her. Too much going on under that messy red hair. Was she the reason why he never liked redheads? Then, too, there was that time in Burger King when Betty Anne had flirted him out of his mind, mocked him for falling for it, then brazenly left with another boy. Jack had barely had time to suffer the humiliation when Foxx had done a remarkable imitation of Betty Anne purring like Marilyn Monroe in a sexy-seductive strip-tease-like dance that had everyone laughing, even Jack. She was so captivating, he saw her in a whole new way, astonishing himself at the suddenness of this switch. He'd caught up with her later, walked her home, them both singing "Row row row your boat" like a couple of silly kids until after three rounds of it, he stopped singing and drew her to him, kissing her, surprised that she didn't protest, not until he actually became overwhelmed by desire. "No, please," she kept saying, trying to push him off. Unable to contain his ardor, he'd pulled her down to the soft cool evening grass covering her mouth with kisses, excited beyond his capacity to control until he came in his pants like the idiot adolescent she had always taken him to be. He was so ashamed, he couldn't apologize. He couldn't even look at her. When he'd seen her a few weeks later at the high school prom, she was dressed up in a beautiful party gown, an orchid pinned on her shoulder. Without her large round glasses, she wasn't Foxx at all but a smiling, lovely-looking girl. He tried to catch her eyes, hoping she would smile at him, but it never happened. He

wondered whom she had come with, then avoided trying to find out.
He'd never seen her again until now.

"But Cyrus is dead, Jack. You came home and Cyrus is dead."

"What's that supposed to mean?"

"The arm bone connected to the shoulder bone," she sang a line of
the old spiritual.

"I know the song, Foxx. What I heard was that Cyrus had got
himself in trouble a lot."

"Sure, he was bad. All those rotten things they say on Clark Street.
Like he beat up on Ruby. Blacks are always killing each other, it's amaz-
ing how there are so many of them left." Then all the sarcasm dissolved
into pain. "Cyrus was a good guy, Jack."

From her tone, he understood her to mean a lot more than that.
All this was beating her down and she wanted to be free of it.

"Why don't you just go, Jack. You shouldn't have come back. You
don't belong here anymore. Just look at that limo! Jesus, what's it doing
in Gandee? Why it's bigger than our high school! Does it have a toilet?
A jacuzzi, maybe? It goes with your woman, doesn't it. And your money
man. And worst of all, it goes with you. Tell me something, Jack: when
you look in the mirror, who do you see? Do you see anyone you know,
Jack?"

"You're weird, Foxx. You're really weird."

She stared at him, her eyes a mixture of pity and contempt.

"What are you, Jack?"

Then there was Gordon, pushing his bulky way through all those
bodies, moving as quickly as he could without seeming to, carefully
concealing his urgency. Gordon had him firmly by the arm, mumbling
in his ears "Let's go, let's go!" As though every second mattered. He
hustled Jack to the rear door of the limo, then slammed it behind him,
and Jack was instantly bathed in quadraphonic sounds and sensuous
perfume, and off they went.

"Well, I'm tellin' you kids, *we're out of here!*" Gordon said. "Friggin'
murder," Gordon said, wiping his face with a huge handkerchief. It was
the first time Jack had ever seen Gordon sweat. "Goddam, it could've
gotten real messy. Your high school catcher! Good God!"

"Who was the raggedy redhead?" Judith asked.

"You don't want to know," said Jack, sounding like it was such an
obscenity, any further mention was out of the question. He put his arm
around her and drew her closer, less for her comfort than for his own.

"You might as well know this, Jack," she sighed at the confession she was about to make. "I'm sorry but I don't like being around poor people. Especially the colored. If I were colored and poor, I think I'd just die!" Then, as an afterthought: "I'll tell you something else: I don't care how people make their money. Not any more. The only thing that counts is having it!"

He was at the brass knobs of the bar cabinet in front of him, eager to celebrate. Not a toilet but a bar, he mused. He poured two stiff drinks of bourbon. As a rule, Gordon didn't drink but Judith did.

Then, surprisingly he asked for one for himself. "Make it a double, if you don't mind."

Gordon drank like a man with a purpose, large substantial swallows that fueled his intensity.

"*I'll* tell you something, kid. This could've been one hell of a mess. If the TV had got to that murder site, the whole show would've gone down the drain. Your battery mate! Jesus. You can thank your Uncle Sam for holding them off!"

He held up his glass as if in a toast to Sam.

"I'll tell you something else, kid. You can forget about that murder. It counts for nothing in your life. Your father told me, it happens so much, they can't solve them half the time. What I'm gettin' at, the opening of the ball park was great. A lot of people are going to appreciate what you gave this town, especially the black kids. The rest of what happened, forget it!"

He handed his empty glass back for a refill, bubbling over with a need to keep talking.

"We're gettin' out of here, kid," Gordon went on. "You can call your folks from St. Louis. We're goin' straight to New York. Sorry, kid, but it's the smart thing to do."

Jack was anything but sorry. He had no desire to spend time with his folks, certainly not with Judith along. He couldn't get out of Gandee quickly enough. He raised his glass in a toast to New York.

"I love it!" he said.

Tina Turner's CD was jumping with "Paradise Is Here."

And Judith's hand was on his thigh again.

New York with Judith was a special treat. Leaving Gandee for the Plaza Hotel was like moving from a garbage dump into a palace. The bellhop had hardly left their suite when she drew him into the bedroom and they went at each other like a pair of long lost lovers. Judith could take the kid out of Gandee and make him forget he had ever been there. The city was an aphrodisiac while the Plaza added dignity to their passions.

He had never before spent full time with any woman, never really believed that the magic could be sustained. He had always been intimidated by New York, moving from the Roosevelt Hotel to Shea Stadium and back like a commuter, concentrating on baseball as if the city were a hostile distraction that would threaten his performance. Corky would take him to Smith and Walensky's for steak dinner and laugh at his reluctance to go elsewhere. Judith, however, liberated him. She introduced him to exotic restaurants, took him to *Ragtime* on Broadway, to jazz at the Blue Note, one treat segueing into another. With Judith, fun was built into living. Life had no other function than seeking pleasure. When she spoke of her history, nothing that ever happened to her was so sacred that she couldn't make mockery of it. As she recounted the end of her marriage, she made it sound like a sitcom: bored at another formal dinner by her husband's endless stockbroker bullshit, she simply rose from the table to dance a striptease around them, then jiggled out the door and filed for divorce in the morning. On another day at breakfast, she told about an affair she'd had at Bryn Mawr with her handsome blue-eyed married professor of

English lit. Since all the girls adored him, she had to have him. She seduced him with a double-edged sword, writing suggestive essays on romantic poetry, beguiling him with her own sexual fantasies. She had him before he knew it. The more he resisted her, the more elusive she became, playing the old game of backing off until she caught him. The tease was consummated, finally, on a blanket in the back of his station wagon and escalated through the soft Pennsylvania spring to a week-end tryst in a Philadelphia hotel. She was barely eighteen but his declaration of love for her was the triumph of her already adventurous life. After all, he had a wife and two children. So she'd ended the affair, taking new pleasure in the way it tortured him. Then, one day in late May, he had to see her, he told her his marriage had become a nightmare, he loved only her, he wanted to *marry her!* Now that she had gone beyond victory, the young student told the middle-aged professor that he was a fool. Less than a week later, he'd jumped off the roof of that same Philadelphia hotel. She ran these two stories together with a continuing insouciance. There was no resentment in Judith, no remorse. She simply danced away from whatever displeased her, always in control, always delighting in the impact of her beauty. She could be aloof as when he had first met her in the children's hospital in Los Angeles, then sparkling like a Roman Candle when he'd seen her next, months later, at a Sunday afternoon at Dodgers Stadium. Walking to the dugout after his pre-game warm-up there she was in the VIP box, golden hair sparkling in the sun above a bright green sweater, and beside her, a twelve-year-old boy in a leg cast in a wheelchair.

"Well, hello again," she'd said.

He never spoke to spectators. He never so much as acknowledged their existence. This time, however, he couldn't believe his eyes.

"Meet Clifton," she said.

He nodded. "You sure hang out with good-looking women, Clifton," he said.

"She sure gets the best seats," replied the kid.

Jack tossed him the warm-up ball, and that was the end of it.

Between innings, he'd avoided glancing at her as he came off the mound, a ritual work ethic never to be violated, but he never forgot that she was there. In the eighth inning, he put on his warm-up jacket, hands in slashed pockets, and he felt a folded piece of score card. He didn't have to look, he knew it was a note from her. The message read: "I love breakfast."

Three little words that had changed his life.

In New York now, there too was Gordon, forever in pursuit of lucrative new ventures: a million-dollar book publishing deal, a new Black Jack sports shoe to be manufactured in the Philippine Islands, more dog food commercials.

Then, too, Ted Pagonis was in town for the World Series and insisted that Jack have lunch with him. Their meeting was at the Cosmopolitan Club where the rich and super rich came together like brothers, where the bar, card room, restaurant, game room, and library were visited (in that order). Pagonis was waiting for him in the game room, knocking in pool shots like one who had spent his life in pool parlors, not board rooms. His slender wrists were exposed from rolled-up sleeves, bow tie intact, broad white suspenders over white-on-white shirt. Behind him, the TV rolled stock market prices under a soundless sound track. An black servant tended a small wet bar in the corner.

"You shoot pool, kid?"

Pagonis's greeting was a bold-faced challenge. The tycoon was obviously a competitor down to his fingertips. Whatever the real reason for this luncheon, he first wanted to whip Jack in a demonstration of his talent beyond the power of his wealth.

"Good to see you, sir." Jack's defense was to be as polite as Pagonis was brash.

"You didn't answer my question, kid."

Pagonis had always called him Jack. Was "kid" intended to demean him?

"Yes, sir. I shoot pool."

Since he'd first visited D.D.'s Tavern as a teen-ager, he'd played eight ball for as long as he could hold the table. Then, as a big leaguer, he'd been inspired by his old roommate Corky at the best pool parlors. "The still ball, Roomie: it calls for the best hand-to-eye coordination. Concentration, control of nerves, steady breathing. You hear what I'm sayin'?"

Jack heard. The same words applied to pitching, all the way back to Cyrus behind that Shell station.

"I figured," said Pagonis. "Grab a stick while I take a leak. Thomas, give Mr. Cagle a beer."

It was the finest table Jack had ever played on. Smooth, fast roll, lively cushions, pockets that seemed virgin. It was inspiring.

"A small wager, kid? Five grand, maybe?"

Jack smiled. Why not? The number was irrelevant. Only the challenge mattered to him.

"Well, sir, I seldom bet less than ten." An out-and-out lie, but the moment cried out for defiance.

"Suppose we go to twenty, kid."

"Twenty is fine, sir."

"Rack 'em up, Thomas!"

They played safe shots until Jack saw a combination shot that might work. He circled the table twice like a professional golfer lining up a treacherous side-of-hill putt. A gamble, yes, but he liked the odds.

"Three ball in the corner, sir."

He then scattered the pile and watched the three ball drop as if it had eyes. For openers, as good as it gets. Pagonis's comment, however, was anything but.

"If you're thinking of marrying my daughter, kid, forget it."

The words came out of nowhere, it seemed. Jack pretended that he hadn't heard, circling the table as he lined up the open shots that would be like shooting fish in a barrel.

What in hell was Pagonis talking about?

"She's trouble, kid. Bad trouble."

Jack heard him; it was like the rumbling of thunder.

"She's a man-eater. She'll chew you up and spit out the hairs. It's her mission in life, kid, and she's the best there is."

Jack had no need to face those beady eyes. He tried to believe that the man was joking but he could hear no whimsy. Even the whip-like "kid" had a special sting to it. In the periphery of his vision, he saw the match light up the cigar, immediately smelling the pungent aroma; fine tobacco or not, cigars always made him sick.

"She's got all the right tools. And let me tell you, she practices, stands in the middle of three mirrors and shakes her gorgeous little ass in a variety of moves, small, medium, and large, ready for use on all occasions. Subtle stuff, sexy as all get out. Like her perfume. You like that scent, kid? Secret ingredients to excite the male hormones. She went special to India for it, custom-conceived to blend with her own body smell, would you believe it?"

Jack sipped beer as he walked around the table, looking for all the world like a man who was stone deaf.

"She tell you about the teacher at Bryn Mawr? Ha, you bet she did. She's proud of it. You catch that, kid? She can drive a man to jump off a roof!"

Jack positioned himself for the next shot with the cool of a safe-cracker, then rammed two more balls in the same pocket, enjoying the crisp sound of their dropping.

"You're thinking what a great year you had, how she makes you a winner. But that was the fun-and-games part. No commitments, everybody's loose, you follow me, kid? But if you marry her, she'll cut you to ribbons!

"You don't seem to be getting my message. You think maybe I'm jokin', eh? You think I'd joke about something like this? Makes you wonder, don't it?"

Jack wondered, all right. He didn't look up, knowing that if he did, he'd seem all the more stupid for not replying. What could he say? He never could deal with this kind of shit. He didn't have the quick tongue like Corky's. His stomach was doing the talking, rumbling from the power of Pagonis's challenge. Like being backed into a corner, he thought. If it wasn't one father it was another. He stared at the pool table looking for a way out among the spread of balls. He would hide behind his pool shots. He had to keep on shooting. He couldn't miss. Take his time. Concentrate. They were in separate worlds. As he moved by the servant, he even smiled, a pretense at his indifference to all that was being said. And to prove it, he rapped his eighth consecutive shot the length of the table, squarely into the corner pocket.

Jack paused to sip his beer, relieved at its cool passage down his gullet. No sooner had he emptied the stein when Thomas was there with another.

"That hundred-million-dollar contract is the name of this game, kid. You turn out to be a limp dick, I could lose the franchise. You follow me? I'm saying, if you marry my daughter *you're as good as dead!*"

Well, there it was. The snarling cat was out of the bag. People killed for a small percentage of that. To Judith, though, all money was play money. To Pagonis, Judith's game was daughter versus father, whoever gets the last laugh wins. Jack had never heard anything like it. Pagonis had brought him here not to shoot pool but to dump on him. It made sense. It made no sense. It was madness. What did Pagonis think might happen? Was Judith going to fuck him to death?

There were five balls left on the table. No small achievement, for Jack had never been this close to running a rack. He felt a rush of adrenalin, the tangle of hot nerve endings, fierce demands on his hunger to win. Had all this bullshit about Judith somehow inspired him? He studied his next shot, and the one after. He got behind the cue ball and studied the angles.

More than all else he wanted to run the table. He stepped back to take a deep breath. As he lined up his next shot, suddenly, behind his back, he heard a soft guttural throat-clearing. A warning from Thomas. He backed off to rechalk his cue tip and saw what Thomas had seen: the danger of scratching. Immediately, he moved around the table for a different play, took another deep breath, then cut it neatly into a side pocket. Quickly, then, before he could doubt himself, he knocked in another. The prospect of going the whole way now seemed real. He would not be distracted. He zeroed in on what he had to do. Two more shots. It was all that mattered. Two more goddam pool shots and he would be king of the world.

"In her high school year book, kid, class of '89—Biggest Flirt: Judith Pagonis. Also, but not listed: Biggest Liar. She tells it like it is or tells it like it isn't, but she doesn't know the difference and neither will you!"

The penultimate shot was hanging on the lip of a side pocket demanding a soft kiss from a treacherous angle. But kiss it he did, and it fell sweetly into its hole. Then the bad news was waiting for him for he had left the cue ball clinging to the distant felt edge of the rail as if it were magnetized. His last shot would be one mean sonovabitch.

"You marry that bitch, kid, you'll never know what hit you!"

Jack was left with a realization of how great was his resentment. He wanted to tell Pagonis he was going to make this shot then shove the cue stick up his ass. He would rejoice in this declaration of defiance. It would be Jack Clyde Cagle Jr. roaring in the face of wealth and authority with a rousing absurdity.

At the table, he set up the shot oblivious to anything Pagonis might say to him. He laid his right hand on the rail, fingers curling over the stick. His feet were firmly planted as his body braced for the shot. Then he executed, watched the long roll across the felt until the ball fell tenderly into the corner pocket. He'd made it! He'd run the goddam table! He reached for his beer, loving the prospect of seeing Pagonis's humiliation. But when he turned to gloat, Pagonis was not suffering. He was in fact, all smiles, shaking his head like one who had just witnessed a miracle.

"Lemme tell you something, kid. I was a goddam good college tennis player, but I'd get to a tie-breaker and fall apart. 'Shit-in-the-blood,' my coach said. When you first came up, I wondered about you, a punk kid from a dingy little town, a hard-assed war hero father who told me how *he* made you, passed on the hero genes, everyone said. You want to know something? That's all bullshit. Just by looking at you. I could see you're not a hero type. I had the glasses on you one game, tough moment in the ninth, you were so scared you didn't know whether to shit or go blind. You went to the resin bag, and when you turned back you were smiling! All that fear . . . pfft! Gone! What was that, kid? All I knew was that you've got something special from somewhere, like when you run a pool table without half knowing how to hold a cue stick. It takes a fire in the belly, kid. That's what makes you the one.

"I concede, kid. I'll buy you lunch with a twenty-thousand-dollar dessert."

Pagonis took his arm and led him into the dining room, smiling as if he were the one who won the pool game.

Not just twenty grand, as it turned out, but VIP box seats to the World Series opener that night. It was Jack's first visit to Yankee Stadium as well as his first time at a Series game. His entrance with Judith, ten minutes before game time, was greeted with cheers and wolf whistles as they sat beside the Yankee dugout.

"My fastball and your curves," he quipped.

"The whistles were louder," she teased him.

The stadium, meanwhile, had him tingling with its awesome history.

"Babe Ruth!" he said, pointing to right field.

"He'd never hit your fastball, Jack."

"He could hit anyone."

"Really? If he played today, how many homers would he hit?"

"Oh, two or three," he replied.

"Two or three! What's so great about that?"

"Well, he'd be over a hundred years old, Judith." He laughed, then apologized. "Sorry. Old joke."

All jokes ended when the Yankees ran onto the field to crowd sounds louder than anything he had ever heard. As he watched David Cone walk to the mound his throat tightened with envy. What could possibly be a greater challenge than this? Three outs later, he'd be feeling the same thing for Greg Maddux.

Cone, meanwhile, could not be better. Everything he threw was around the plate. He was ahead of every hitter. He had the crowd on its feet repeatedly, yelling for strikeouts. After five innings, no Atlanta hitter got passed second base.

Maddux, meanwhile, held the Yankees scoreless but was in trouble every inning. Jack could see him working hard. Always poised, reaching back for something extra, especially against the middle of the Yankee order. Three double plays ended threatening rallies. Outfielders robbed hitters of extra base hits. Jack loved the tension of a scoreless game.

Cone continued to be masterful through the sixth, striking out his seventh hitter for the third out. Jack watched him leave the mound, enjoying the sight of him enjoying himself. When Maddux took the mound the crowd sensed that this would be the Yankee breakthrough for he had gone to the well too many times.

Maddux, however, had other ideas. He kept the ball down, mixed fast balls with sliders, changed speeds, always working the corners. For the first time, he threw only twelve pitches and retired the side. Jack stood up to applaud him as he left the mound, sensing the magic of unpredictable forces. Was Maddux getting stronger? Would Cone start making mistakes? How long could this marvelous game remain scoreless?

Sure enough, it was Cone's turn to get into trouble. A broken bat single by the leadoff man, then a routine double play ground ball bad-hopped over Brosius's glove, and all of a sudden, the Braves had runners at the corners with none out. Jack was amused to see Cone smiling at Brosius. He got back on the mound, the crowd demanding strikeouts, but everyone in the ball park knew that anything was likely to happen now. Jack knew the feeling. You threw your best stuff and hoped that it worked. Sure enough, Cone popped up the next hitter, then another strikeout got the second out. Then Paul O'Neill pulled down a long fly ball in the right field corner to end the inning. Cone came back to the dugout all smiles and Jack applauded as he once again came to his feet. The crowd did not stop roaring as Maddux walked to the mound to face the Yankees in the bottom of the seventh.

Jack turned to Judith, suddenly aware that he'd barely paid attention to her.

"This is what it's all about, baby," he said. Though he had never said anything truer he felt foolish saying it to her. Nothing could possibly describe the tension of this game.

"It's raining, Jack." Judith curled her voice around the words as if she were delivering message of doom.

A drop, yes. Then another. But to mention rain at this moment was like interrupting great sex to answer a telephone. He leaned over the railing to get nearer to the action, pretending he hadn't heard her complaint.

Maddux threw eight pitches to Jeter before he finally walked him. O'Neill worked the count to full then struck out swinging as Jeter stole second. Judith was looking up at the lights, pointing to the rain.

"Jack!"

With first base open, Maddux intentionally walked Williams, hoping for another double play. Then Tino Martinez beat out a swinging bunt and the bases were loaded.

"Jack, it's really raining!"

He took off his jacket, draped it over her head and shoulders. There was a conference on the mound while the crowd roared for action. How could he possibly leave now? He had become Maddux himself, the man at the heart of the crisis. This was his ball game to win or lose. What could a few drops of rain matter at such a moment?

"Jack, this is dumb! I'll get soaked!"

Soaked? It was barely dripping. The drama meant nothing to her. She cared about a threat to her hair. She couldn't even see why any of what was happening on the field could mean anything to him. She didn't want to be here in the first place. In her purse were unused tickets to *Chicago*, another musical for which she'd had her hair done that afternoon. She'd given way to be nice to him, but now she wanted to leave.

He got the message, all right. Suddenly he wasn't Greg Maddux any longer. At this moment he wasn't even Black Jack Cagle. He was Judith's lover which was no small thing, and best he pay heed to that. Maddux would stay in the game, but Judith would not. He even sensed that she would leave without him, take their waiting limo back to the Plaza and feel perfectly justified in doing so.

For all his desire to stay, he was more afraid of the consequences.

"Hey!" he smiled at her. "We'll beat the traffic!"

He never looked back. He knew that all eyes were on them. He could even feel the TV camera panning with them, the announcers would be having a field day.

In the limo, he turned on the radio, not for the end of the game, but to the music she liked. Anything less might suggest his frustration. He even hoped it would begin to really rain, if only to make her feel better about leaving. But it didn't. Quite the opposite, in fact, the more apparent when the chauffeur turned off the wipers. Just to show that he held no resentment, he took her hand and began to caress her fin-

gers, one by one. "Fiveplay," she once called it, and her smile now promised a reward for his deference. The day would end in a glorious display
of passion. Judith could do what Maddux could not. Nothing need be
said. He looked out at the passing city scene and let the sound of music
take over.

In their suite, she kissed him then disappeared into the bathroom.
Immediately he thought of catching the end of the ball game on TV
but pictured her coming out of a quick pre-sex shower to face that
again. ("Well, if you'd rather watch *that*.") Then he heard tub water
sounds, but it was too late, and he settled for a movie as he undressed.

She came out of the bathroom nude but for the turbaned towel on
her head. She stood at the bedroom door mirror, adjusting the angle so
he could have both a front and rear view simultaneously. She saw his
delight and smiled. Then, as she walked to the bed, she stopped to kiss
him on the top of the forehead, patting his cheek like a visiting aunt.

"Watch the movie. It's okay," she said.

"What!"

"I really don't feel like it." Then, with a sympathetic smile: "Sorry."

The words stunned him as if she had slapped his face. It was so
startling, he thought that she might just be teasing him in a new kind
of foreplay wherein she would take him from shock to ecstasy in quick
flip flops. He grabbed her arm and drew her to him, kissing her with an
eagerness that would turn the tease into desire. But when she pushed
away, it was a definite no. He couldn't understand this. She was enjoying his frustration, punishing him. For what? For making her go to the
game? For not leaving at the first drop of rain? "Sorry," she'd said and
danced away in triumph, pulled back the bedcovers, and disappeared
under them like a curtain falling on the last act.

"I really don't feel like it," she said. But *he* did. He had earned that
right, by God. She was playing games with him. ("She's a man-eater,
kid. She'll eat you alive!") She had made him leave the ball game, where
he most wanted to be, and now, to compound her victory, she would
deny him what he most wanted to do.

He wasn't going to let her get away with that. As if to prove that he
was in control of himself, he took his time about making his move. He
washed his face and brushed his teeth, then walked calmly to the bed,
pulled off the covers and took her in his arms. His hands kneaded her
flesh, buttocks to thighs, as she tried to stop him. She didn't have a
chance. In time, he drew her legs apart and took her, kissing her ear
because that excited her the most. Inevitably, she abandoned herself,

moaning as she thrashed under him until they both were spent. It wasn't love by a long shot but it was better than rejection. When it was over, he chose to kiss her goodnight, but he should have known better.

"Damn you!" she muttered and rose from the bed, taking a pillow and blanket with her to bed down on the huge living room sofa. And because she had never done that before, he hated it all the more.

Alone, there was no way he could fall asleep. In minutes, he was out of bed, nursing his defeat under a fresh wave of helplessness. He'd made a fool of himself, all right, but he couldn't understand the nature of his folly. In the bathroom mirror, the sight of his face in triptych seemed like a living mug shot. His Fu Manchu moustache seemed preposterous. He didn't look mean, he looked pathetic. His eyes were watery-sad like one drained of passion and left with shame. He didn't like his eyes staring back at him. When he was a teenager with acne, he hated all mirrors. Even when he finally passed through those tortured years, he disliked what he saw. Since his father had always made him feel stupid, Jack had grown up seeing the stupid face of a loser. Like the night he'd gotten all dressed up to take Betty Anne to the movies but his father had stopped him. "You didn't clean out the garage!" When he finally picked her up, Betty Anne took one look—and smell—and cried out in disgust. "God, you're vile!" It was her favorite word. In the foyer mirror, he saw the greasy smudges on his cheeks and the residue of oil on his pants. Sure he could've cleaned up but he'd wanted to blame his father for the way she scorned him. He hated that memory, another assault on his shakiness. In defiance, he glared at the mirror with a variety of furious Black Jack game faces to see what *that* looked like.

("When you look in a mirror, do you see anything at all?" Foxx had chided him.)

He turned away, wondering at this morbid mood swing. Then he saw the pastel blue telephone hanging beside the toilet, an enticement he couldn't refuse. His first thought was to call Corky. He needed Corky now.

"Thomas J. Corcoran, here."

"It's me."

"Hey, last I saw, you were tossing a baseball to a sheriff. TV man said it was a hundred-miles-an-hour in slow mo."

"Well, I am now at the Plaza." Jack came on like the king of the world, itemizing the New York City goodies he had experienced over the last few days.

"Okay, okay," Corky broke in. "Everything is terrific. My kid says you must be okay 'cause you haven't called. So what's the problem now?"

"Problem? Man, I'm on a beautiful roll!"

"Somehow it crossed my mind that maybe Judith was busting your balls."

"You sound just like her father."

"That so? Must've been a helluva lunch, you two. I always thought he had mixed paternal feelings about her."

"Judith couldn't care less."

"Sure. Judith loves Judith."

"C'mon, she's more complicated than that. She just likes to play the princess. I really think she loves me, Corky. I was thinking, maybe I love her."

Jack's ear rang with what he took to be a stunned silence.

"Roomie, you don't know what the words mean."

"Hey, I'm twenty-seven. Guys are supposed to be married at twenty-seven."

"Wait five years, Roomie. If it's with Judith, wait ten." Then, quickly: "You better be joking."

"I'll tell you something else: her father really likes me."

"He likes your left arm. He never thinks about the rest of you."

"Corky, sometimes . . . Jesus!"

"Sometimes what?"

"You can be a real downer, you know?"

"You want an upper? Okay, man, you're the greatest. Everybody loves you because you're such a neat guy."

"Oh for Chrissake!"

"Look! Just don't marry her. Don't even consider marrying her. If you find a wedding ring in your pocket, stick it in your nose. You hear what I'm sayin', Roomie?"

"Fuck you, Corky."

The whole interplay had escalated out of control. He was humiliated by his own anger, especially since he'd brought the whole thing down on himself. Jack had been asking for it, and Corky had responded.

"Hey, Corky, I'm sorry."

Another silence on the line, almost as if the phones went dead. Jack was about to apologize again when he heard the sigh.

"What's happenin', Roomie? You having an attack of 'off-season stress syndrome?' I'm thinking that somethin' happened in Gandee. Hey, man, did somethin' happen in Gandee?"

Jack winced. When he rallied, he came on with the subtlety of a
kid caught with his hand in the cookie jar.

"Gandee? Never heard of it. You sure you got that name right?"

Corky knew when to quit.

"Take two and hit to right, man, you can't lose."

Famous last words. Corky hung up leaving him to dangle in doubt.

What had happened in Gandee? Jack was hurting. The sound of
those words left a sediment of guilt on his psyche. He could keep the
secret from Corky but he couldn't keep it from himself. The memory of
Cyrus's bloody body was bound to haunt him. And Ruby's eyes boring
into him, pegging him for a phony, right from the beginning. He would
never get over that either.

He couldn't call Cyrus, but he could call Ruby. Without knowing
what he would say to her? His head was spinning with "what-ifs," suddenly realizing that in all the years he'd never called Cyrus, not once.
Could he now call Ruby?

He called information, Gandee. Cyrus Coles on Clark Street. And
when he dialed the number he held his breath as it rang. Once, twice,
three times, promising himself he would hang up after the fourth ring.

Then a man answered.

"Yeah?"

"Is Ruby there, please? This is Jack Cagle."

"Whattaya want?" Then: "Who?"

"Jack Cagle."

"Hey, you still around?"

"No. Who is this?"

"Lukas, man."

"Hey, Lukas." Ruby's brother, Jack remembered. "Ruby there?"

"Shit, no. She in *jail*, man!"

"*In jail*? How come?"

"Murder one. They say she killed him."

"What! Killed who?"

"Cyrus, man! The fuckers say she killed him!"

"Jesus, Lukas. What in hell is goin' on!"

"You askin' me? Ask your fuckin' daddy!" Lukas's rage came at him
across a thousand miles. "It weren't an hour after we put Cyrus under
when they come for her. They lock her up, they don't say nothin'!"

"I'm sorry, Lukas. I didn't know."

"J.C., you don't know shit."

Jack sat on the lid in a sudden sweat, picturing his father taking
Ruby away. Where had Jack been at that moment? Having lunch at

Lutece? Making big money deals with Gordon? Shooting pool with Pagonis? Fucking Judith between satin sheets? The pounding in his skull became fierce. He pressed fingers against his temples to contain it, all the while seeing Ruby looking daggers at him again, demanding something from him that frightened him. What could he do?

It would take a lot of bourbon to get him through the night.

Without knowing how it came to be morning, Jack heard and smelled room service breakfast in the living room. Judith was at the table, sipping coffee over the *New York Times*.

"Yankees won in the ninth," she said. "One zip."

She was happy to tell him the news as if nothing had happened last night to find her otherwise. She poured coffee for him and handed him the sports section. Under the silver dome there were poached eggs on English muffins with a side order of sausages. She was smiling at him, contented with her multiple victories. He was being pardoned, he guessed; she had punished him enough. Her seductive smile even suggested a bedding after breakfast if he played his cards right.

"There's some bad news," he told her. "Seems like they arrested Ruby Coles for that murder."

Since this came at her out of the blue, Judith was baffled.

"What?" she said.

"I called, spoke to her brother," he said.

"Oh? Why'd you do that?"

"I wanted to talk to her. To see how she was and all."

"I don't understand, Jack." Her tone was loaded with displeasure. Why would he want to talk to that woman?

"I was thinking, Judith. Maybe I ought to go back there."

"What! To that town?" She made a face, unable to say its name. "What in hell for?"

"She didn't kill him, Judith."

48

"You're not making sense. If they put her in jail, they must have something on her."

"Whatever, she didn't kill him."

Immediately, she was all over him.

"If you go back, what are you going to accomplish? What could you possibly do? Why don't you call your father? Wouldn't he know everything about it? What could you be gaining? Can't you take care of it on the phone?" She became so convinced by her suggestions, she practically picked up the phone for him.

"I suppose," he said, then counterattacked. "But it wouldn't be the same. She's in jail for murder, Judith!"

"I heard you. What I haven't heard is what that's got to do with you!"

He didn't know how to answer, only that he had to make a stand. Fumbling with unspoken words, he finally blurted out "I owe her!" startling himself as much as he startled her. Immediately, he regretted it. She stared at him, sensing an advantage, and went right at him.

"You owe her? You owe her what? Jack, I don't understand!"

He wasn't about to explain. Details about Cyrus and the Shell station were his private memories, much too painful to deal with now.

"Well, I owe her to go back," he said, aware of how feeble it sounded. "She needs help. Okay? I need to do this, Judith."

She kept shaking her head in continuing denial.

"You can do everything by phone, Jack. Your father is sheriff, your uncle is mayor. So call. Find out. I can't for the life of me see what good it would do to go back. Do whatever you can. But to go back?" Her voice shifted to compassion. "Jack, it will just frustrate you."

He liked his resistance for it reassured him, saving him from an overlay of guilt. Even more, he liked that she argued, especially since he really agreed with her. Whatever happened in that long night of agony, she had turned the morning into a big relief.

He smiled at her finally, nodding his appreciation.

"Yeah. Guess you're right," he said.

"Jack . . ." She leaned over to kiss him. "Sometimes you can be such a fool!" It was her declaration of peacemaking after a victory. And the way she saw it, since he had played his cards right after all, she rewarded him by taking his hand and leading him back to the bedroom.

Afterward, they lay quietly like two spoons. The seesaw had temporarily stopped at level though it was her feet that held it there, not his. The image teased him. There was never any ground under his feet, was there? At such moments, he took to counting his blessings. He was good at that. They were numerous and reassuring for they always rode herd over the occasional dark forces that lurked in the corners of his mind. He reconsidered the Ruby matter without pain. He would talk to his father, send whatever money was appropriate. It was as Judith pointed out, no one would expect any more from him. He turned his thoughts to the pleasures of New York during the rest of the week, and then, what? Japan? Like Gordon had said, he'd have a catch with the emperor with Judith watching in a kimono.

Then he heard her voice in the pillow, muffled and distant and terribly earnest.

"I've been thinking, Jack."

"Oh?"

"Maybe you *should* go back."

"What? To Gandee?"

"Everything was so mixed up last night," she persisted. "I really didn't understand. You know something?"

"What?"

"You're beautiful, Jack. The way you want to help that poor woman. I didn't know that it mattered to you. It does, doesn't it?"

"I guess. Sure."

"Well, that makes you special."

"But then, like you said, what good would it do?"

"That's not what's important. You'll do what you can. I mean, if you don't go, you'll feel like you should've gone. You get what I mean? This way, you'll be getting it out of your system."

"Yeah," he said.

"You should do it, Jack."

The seesaw was moving again.

"I'm proud of you," she murmured.

No limo this time. He rented a red Taurus at the St. Louis airport, wore dark shades under a cowboy hat to avoid recognition. Eyes front, quick paces, he got by without incident. For Jack, to be alone was no small thing. To take on the living world without an ally, without Gordon, without Judith, was like walking to the mound without his glove. En route back to Gandee, he had not the slightest notion as to what he was going to do. He became so smothered by an accumulation of doubts, he considered turning back. Swing around, back to the airport, back into Judith's arms. But he had called his folks to tell them he was coming, briefly explaining why. "Ruby?" His father could not have been more astonished. "What the devil business is this of yours?"

He didn't explain, just reported the time of his arrival. That way, there would be no arguments.

If all you saw in Gandee was its renovated Town Hall, you'd think it was a vibrant community of well-turned-out public-spirited citizens living in harmony. The building itself was over a hundred years old, but there were no apparent signs of decay. As Jack entered, he was amazed, remembering its old tackiness. Dreary glass-bowl lighting from cracked ceilings had been replaced by inset panels. Dominating the bright lobby was a larger-than-life portrait of Mayor Sam Manning himself. On clean white walls, there were historical photographs mounted on mahogany frames of old Gandee. The largest of these was of the Statue of

Colonel Evan Gandee on horseback, that celebrated nineteenth- century Indian fighter, for whom the town was named. Even the old benches were gone. Tiled floors sparkled as if polished daily.

Sam's office was even more plush. Wall-to-wall beige carpeting and matching drapes. The huge desk was polished walnut behind which the walls were covered with photos of Sam in company with a variety of celebrities—including Jack, of course, a pre-game on-the-field shot in Los Angeles.

The mayor rose to greet him. With him were his father and Lem Starger, the black deputy. Two men in suits rose similarly. One was Xavier Norton, the bearded defense attorney, and a tall man, the district attorney, Vincent Hayes, who liked to wear his glasses on the tip of his nose. Sam, cheerful and spirited, was master of the ceremony.

"When your father told me you were coming, we couldn't have been more pleased. You're the one, kid. You alone can make this happen!"

Whatever it was, Jack was happy for the prospect. Sam could make you feel good with one flicker of his eye. He was the ultimate convincer, especially when you wanted to be convinced.

"Nobody wants to put Ruby on trial, kid. For one thing, we don't want to stir up the colored folk. These days it don't take much, believe me. If Ruby got convicted, hey, the town would suffer, and I mean suffer."

Everyone agreed with that.

"So we worked it out, kid. Very simple, clear cut, and legally proper. The killing will be booked as 'justifiable homicide.' Ruby confesses. We suspend sentence. She walks."

"And case dismissed!" said the DA.

"Jack, we need you," The mayor went on. "Xavier here—hey, let me tell you, he's the top public defender in the county. You tell him, Xavier."

"She needs to be convinced, Jack. I see her as a tough nut to crack."

"Even though it's to her advantage!" the mayor emphasized.

"She claims to be innocent, of course," Xavier explained.

Here, Jack could hardly restrain the inevitable challenge. "You mean she's not? You really think she killed him?"

The mayor was ready for him. Sam Manning was a man who was always ready.

"People change, kid. Some make it, some don't. God knows, it ain't easy for black folk, but that's life and there's no way to get around it." Sam was shaking his head, a signal that there was more to come. "What it gets down to, here, like Cyrus, Ruby just ain't the gal you might remember."

"What's that supposed to mean?" Jack asked. "What happened!"

"She ain't all there," Sam explained, making the loony gesture with a finger circling at his temple.

Norton, Ruby's lawyer, took over. "She had what they call an episode. A year or so back, she became, well, suicidal. They put her in a mental hospital." As he spoke, he opened his file folder to report the details. "County General, May 19 to June 1. They had her on Thorazine. Anti-depressant drugs."

"Then there was Cyrus. He, too. He, too."

Jack's head snapped up. "What about Cyrus?" He had to know.

"Tell 'im, Lem." The mayor was good at keeping everyone in the action.

The deputy sheriff cleared his throat, not once but twice, as if to be absolutely certain the words came out properly.

"Cyrus had a record. Twice DWI. Plus substance abuse." Then, the real bad news. Jack could feel it coming. "He had some bad scenes with Ruby. Bad fights. He'd get drunk and slap her around some."

"We got witnesses," Starger went on. "There were repeated incidents."

Here the DA took over. They were bombarding Jack from all sides.

"On the afternoon of the murder, apparently she tried to stop him from going to the ball park. We know that from a neighbor."

"He had on his baseball uniform," Sam said. "And they drove off together in the van."

Details raced through Jack's head. He knew nothing about rules of evidence except what he'd picked up on movies and TV. But what he'd heard here did not get beyond guesswork. No one saw the killing, did they? Didn't they have to have solid evidence? The so-called smoking gun?

The DA came in again. "Cyrus was killed with a shotgun at point blank range. There's got to be more shotguns in Gandee than there are TV sets. If we had to, we could go to trial without a murder weapon."

The mayor kept the momentum going. "There's testimony that Cyrus threatened to beat her up that very afternoon. That's in her favor, kid. We could say, to save herself, she had to shoot him, even if she didn't plan to. *Especially* if she didn't plan to."

Jack looked to Norton for his reaction. As Ruby's lawyer, what did he think of all this?

He nodded, albeit reluctantly. "I'm afraid that's about it. Sure, there are complications. It's never open and shut. Put a witness on the stand, anything can happen. I've seen the DA here practically dismember one of my witnesses. I've got to admit, though, I don't cotton to a trial."

Into the breach stepped the mayor: "The main point of all this is, what's best for everybody. You see that, kid? What's best for everybody?"

Then, with that special something extra, he added: "You can tell her there'll be a job waiting for her at the county seat."

And that was it. The whole ball of wax was neatly packaged. The room fell silent. If not all eyes, for they were too polite to stare at him, then all ears were concentrated on his response. Having spoken, they were smart enough not to go over it again.

Jack summed it up for his own benefit. "You want me to get her to cop a plea." He needed to roll it around in his head, and not wanting to face them, he left his seat for the window. He had always liked windows. There was always something to look at. You could clear your head looking out a window. Here, in the center of the square, the heroic Colonel Gandee on that huge bronze horse seemed to be staring right at him.

These men, important men in the county, official men elected to public office, were putting him in a position to perform a vital public service. He had to respect their perceptions in contrast to his ignorance. And who was he to think he could question them? As the mayor had said: "What's best for everybody?"

Jack could not help but wonder, what was best for *him*?

"What's troubling you, kid?"

Jack wondered out loud: "How come, if you've got enough on her, she don't jump at the offer? I mean, why do you need me?" He turned toward her lawyer. "You advise her? Didn't *you* lay this out so she saw what's best for her?"

"We just discussed this yesterday, Jack. I haven't spoken to her. I was going to, then we heard you were coming."

"Your father's idea, kid," said Sam.

Jack looked at him. His father was the only one standing, leaning against the wall with his arms folded across his chest. He seemed apart from the others, the man of action in a group of policy makers.

"You want to help, Son? It seemed to me, a gal like her, she don't cotton to people in authority. Not many of the colored do. Seemed to me, she'd be more likely to heed what you tell her."

Jack had enough doubts to make his head spin, but maybe he could go to her full of apologies for the way he had failed her. Wouldn't that soften her up? He could turn his remorse into a victory and free him-

self of it at the same time. If he pulled this off, he could picture the
rewards. For one thing, Gordon could make hay of it. And Judith would
adore him all the more. He was pleased with himself for the way he
had challenged them, and having done that, he could better accept
what they wanted him to do. It was, as Sam said, the best thing for
everybody—including himself.

"Okay, Sam," he said. "I'll give it a try."

They all nodded, acting as though they knew he would, and somehow, that pleased him most of all.

His father walked out with him, a big hand on his shoulder. Ap-
proval, by God. Jack was going to resolve a criminal problem that his
father couldn't.

The county jail in Overton, barely twenty minutes from Gandee,
was the oldest building in the county. The visitors' room was a twenty-
four by twenty-four-foot tacky area with one sealed window behind
rusted mesh, an impervious double barrier, for the glass was so filthy, it
performed none of the functions of a window. There were six wooden
tables, several naugahyde chairs around them. Four vending machines
were backed against a wall. Jack sat down, brought his hand to his nose
in a vain effort to block the odor. If you were locked up in here, how
long would it take before it became part of your flesh?

He looked up to see Ruby in a prisoner's drab gray smock. Her
wavy black hair was combed, the single cosmetic left to her. He stood
up to greet her and tried to smile. Her eyes told him not to bother.

"You c'n buy me a Coke," she said while he was still on his feet: it
would save a second or two. For Jack, it was a welcome distraction. The
way she asked, a Coke became more important than anything he might
say to her in greeting.

He brought two cups back to the table. No cans, no bottles, just
paper. She closed her eyes and nursed the cola as if it were nectar,
both hands clasping. And when she finally stared at him, her eyes were
terribly sad. He tried to look at the rest of her face, anything to avoid
her eyes.

"What you doin' here, J.C.?"

"I came to help you."

"You come back from all that partyin' to help me?"

"Well, Lukas said you were—"

"I know what he said."

"You don't belong here, Ruby. This is all wrong."

"Tell me 'bout it."

He told her about his morning's meeting in the mayor's office. He was there to bring her the good news, re-creating the substance of the scene as if it were the solution to her problems. Indeed, he recounted it with such a positive feeling, he was swayed by his own conviction. He wanted to include his apologies but got caught up in the legalities. When he finished, she had emptied the cup. Immediately, he went back to the Coke machine for a refill.

"So, all you've got to do is say yes, Ruby. The lawyer will take care of the rest."

She looked at the Coke bubbles, dipped a finger in and licked it as he waited for her to agree.

"Ruby, take the deal. You go free! The mayor even promised to get you a job."

She sighed as she stared at him, shaking her head with obvious disgust.

"No way!" she snapped.

"Ruby—," he began his protest, but she cut him off.

"Back then, you know what I tell Cyrus about you?" She gave him a few seconds to wonder. "Ain't nothing there, I tell him. Just another whitey with a paper asshole."

"I know, Ruby, I'm sorry about all that."

"J.C., you ain't learned a goddam mother-fuckin' thing!"

Sure. It was beat-on-Black-Jack time. Too many blows shoved him over the edge.

"Goddammit, Ruby, I'm here! So let's cut the bullshit. Maybe if you talk to me, I can do something to help. Either you let me try or I go. I'm not having all that much fun, so what's it gonna be? What?"

"Suppose you tell me, J.C. 'cause I don't have a clue."

"Just start talking to me! I don't know what to think anymore. Tell me what happened so I'll know something. God, at least do that!" She stared at him, biting her lips, then looked away, embarrassed by a sudden fit of coughing. When she subsided, she sat perfectly still as if worried about a recurrence, sighing like one too exhausted to keep fighting.

This time, he saw the softness in her eyes. At least he had broken through the hate. She nodded slowly as she put her hands around the Coke. She sipped slowly, then like one tantalized by the taste, poured it down her throat as if it were nectar. He considered getting her another, but she began to speak with a painful softness.

"Oh, man, what you never knew. All them years, you never knew. Cyrus never forgot about you. When you and him was playing ball together, you filled him with pride, man. I filled him with love. Then Gandee filled him with shit. When you got to be the big man, he watched you pitch on TV, always hollerin' at you, do this, do that, workin' them ball games like he was still behind the plate. He never missed a one. When we had troubles, I said 'Call him!' I pick up the phone and get the number, but he pulls it from me. He's gonna ask you for nothin'. Never a second did he want somethin' from you."

Maybe from the pain, he thought, she stopped, trying to figure out how to go on.

"He got killed goin' to be the catcher for you, one last time. J.C., you coulda come to the funeral! You coulda come. I looked at him in the coffin, I think he knew you wasn't there. Seems like the whole story with you and him was one big sad batch of shit. He's six feet under but it still ain't over. Seems like it ain't never gonna be."

She was fighting back an emotion that would inevitably choke her.

"Oh God, I'm sorry, Ruby."

"Yeah, yeah."

She stared at him with a distant hazy look that made him feel as though he weren't even there. When she spoke again, he could barely hear her, words coming out of her weariness like one who had lived with them so long they had lost their power.

"'Cyrus Coles, Plumber' it says on the van. What's missing, J.C.? You wouldn't know, would you, even though you put it there! It's the key word. 'Cyrus Coles, *Nigger* Plumber!' He goes up and down Clark Street, there ain't a house he didn't fix, no more leaks, toilets don't back up no more, he do his magic all over but he can't do it on Black Jack Field. Gandee is bleedin' to death, no more this, no more that, schools fallin' apart, but here come two million dollars for a ball field. You'd think he'd get *that* job. You'd think Mr. Mayor would say, 'Hey, Cyrus was the catcher, the battery mate. Cyrus made it happen. Give that plumbing contract to Cyrus Coles, Plumber.'

"Man, do they screw Cyrus! They fuck up his van when he says no to kickbacks, put sugar in his gas tank, slash his tires. Then they lie about the bids. They do it the Gandee way. Then the Mayor says, hey, Cyrus, J.C. is coming to the opening. The old battery, Cyrus! You gonna be on national TV! I tell Cyrus, no! They just using him. It's TV time, be nice to niggers time. Black Jack gonna throw the first pitch to the fat black-ass Cyrus for good old Gandee! I say '*No!*'

"We fight about it. He never hit me like the neighbors say. I hit *him!* Two, three times, in his fat belly. He laughs. I love him but I can't get with a black man who ain't got anger."

Jack suffered through every gathering moment. The thought that he could have prevented the tragedy, one phone call to Sam, or even his father, and Cyrus would have had the contract. None of this would have happened.

"It messed me up good," Ruby went on. "They tell you how I flipped out? They love it that I flipped out. Every day, seems like something bad would happen, little things, like spilling the coffee; big things like no money, like busted up hopes. Got so, we're fightn' each other, fightin' over the kids. I woke up one night I couldn't breathe none. Like I was chokin' for no reason. I began to scream, just had to scream. They come for me 'cause I couldn't stop screaming. First the police, then the ambulance. In the hospital, they give me drugs to calm me down. Cyrus, he come see me, cryin' like a big fat baby. He couldn't understand. To me, it ain't so strange. Coupla days maybe, there's the pain, then it goes. 'Nigger pain,' my momma used to say, you see so much sufferin', it don't mean nothin'. White man stub his toe, it hurt him more'n a nigger gettin' his head busted." She hissed through her teeth. "When 'Brother Lem' come for me, I say 'Whatcha come for *me* for?' He give me that dumb nigger face and I see everything I gotta know: *they gonna do whatever they want!* There ain't nothin' they can't do! Ruby Coles kill Cyrus Coles? Sure, she's crazy, remember? Them neighbors all hear her screamin, she's gonna kill him sure as shit! Sheeit, I got neighbors who'll say anything Brother Lem wants 'em to say. Ain't it perfect? Niggers kill niggers. If it ain't a man cuttin' up his woman, it's a woman shootin' her man! This ain't the 'Black Community,' it's the 'Black Disunity!'"

He rose from the table for the Coke machine, as much to get away from her as to get a cool drink. He could feel her eyes burning into the back of his neck as he pumped quarters down the slot. When he came back to the table, he set the filled paper cup in front of her but could not look at her. She ignored the Coke but not his return.

"What you want, J.C.? Thanks for comin'? I don't think so. I thank you for nothin'. What you are, just *one big load of shit!*"

She was on her feet when she finished, ready for the guard to take her back to her cell. She didn't so much as glance at him as she turned away.

He'd forgotten the stench of jail until he made it to the fresh air. On the top step, he paused to take a deep breath when he heard a familiar voice sighing, "My, my, my, my." He turned, and there was the redheaded Foxx, sitting on the stone steps, the humungous shoulder bag beside her.

"Foxx," he said, aware that he must really look stupid. With this woman, the extra crease on his forehead was worth a thousand words.

"Have a seat, Jack. You look a bit shaky."

Not sardonic but sympathetic this time. Her soft smile was blessed by the morning sun. What was she doing here? Not that he was surprised, not really. She was Foxx, who always knew more than she said, unlike others who always said more than they knew. She was here, obviously, because she'd known he was coming. No big secret, was it. She was inside his head again, poking around to stir things up.

"It gets messy, doesn't it," she offered, an acknowledgement of her own confusion as well as his.

It stopped him. He didn't walk off as he'd first intended; he confessed.

"She looked at me like I was a cockroach!"

She nodded. "She didn't kill Cyrus, Jack."

"I know, I know."

"But you tried to get her to cop a plea, didn't you?"

"For her own good. For a deal."

"Jack, Jack . . . that marks her for a murderer. That says to the world what the courthouse gang says she is. It insults her marriage, her hus-

59

band, her children, and most of all, herself." She shook her head. "That's not much of a deal, is it?"

He could see that. He could even see himself as Ruby saw him. The cockroach bit. But he could also see the mayor's side of it. The compromise that settles an otherwise impossible situation.

"Her own lawyer, Foxx."

"The illustrious Xavier L. Norton? He's not Ruby's lawyer, he's *theirs!*"

"Well, they worked out a deal that satisfies everyone," he went on. "They want to help her out. She'd be a free woman."

"It gets *them* off the hook, not Ruby. They won't have to find the real killer. They solve the crime and look compassionate doing it. They can even *feel* virtuous!" She sighed, threw up her hands. "Jack, you were mind-raped in a gang-bang!"

This woman really bothered him. She could play games with his head and never lose. President of the chess club, remember? He didn't know why he argued with her; she was so far ahead of him he felt like a fool. He was tempted to fight back, call her a bully just like the big punks who pick on little guys, only she does it with her mouth. But he didn't. Because he knew she was right.

"Jack, I want to show you something," she said, eager eyes behind those huge round glasses.

She took his arm and led him to her aging Toyota, a car so battered, he hesitated getting in. He could even picture her apartment, or house, wherever she lived, a scattering of junk around a word processor, unmade bed, clothes on the floor, dirty dishes in the sink. In the car, it amazed him that the engine responded at the first turn of the ignition key.

She drove to Black Jack Field, exactly where he least wanted to be, barely a week or so after that evening of horror. There was no one there on this gray morning. The wind blew an old newspaper across the outfield. There was assorted junk on the grandstand seats, hundreds of Black Jack candy wrappers.

"Way back . . . do you remember anything about this spot?" she asked.

"No."

"Carson Road," she reminded him.

"The Carson Paint Company?" he asked.

She nodded.

"What about it?" he asked.

She pointed to the ground. "Right here. The paint factory was right here!"

He looked around to get oriented. Boyhood geographical memories were distant and elusive. He shrugged.

"It burned down four years ago. Biggest fire in local history," she said. Then: "Can you imagine how much paint, how many barrels of chemicals, how much toxic filth filtered into this ground? Can you imagine how much toxic waste Carson dumped here *before* that fire. Can you imagine what poisons are stewing under this outfield sod?"

He could, and he couldn't. How could they possibly build a ball field for kids on toxic ground? "Hey, they must have tested it first," he countered. "That stuff dissolves in time, doesn't it?"

"Well, I sure *hope* so. You wouldn't think they'd want to endanger kids, now would they?"

If she wanted to leave him wondering, she sure as hell did.

She then led him to the bathrooms under the stands. The ladies' room showed a puddle oozing from a toilet stall. The toilet itself was clogged. The room smelled with a mixture of human waste and chemical deodorant. She didn't remind him that this was practically brand new.

"It's awful," he said. "How come they don't fix it?"

"I guess they didn't know you were coming." Foxx was bitter again. He even saw her look of mockery, like one who had seen this so many times before she went way beyond disgust. Was she really enjoying this? He used to have a dream in which an umpire refused to make strike calls and kept grinning at him from behind the mask. Now he had the feeling she had her shopping list at the ready. She would go on for hours sticking these pins in him. Outside again, she pointed up at the light tower in left field.

"Two bulbs out already."

He saw the burnt cracked glass, remembered the popping sound when he himself first threw the switch.

"Two more behind home plate," she went on.

He was tired of all this and didn't bother to look.

"It's all about caring, Jack. They built this ball field, nobody cared. From start to finish, they were just making deals."

He didn't want to hear this. He didn't want to hear anything Foxx had to say. Why should he care, anyway? What good would it do? So the goddam field wasn't perfect. So what? Whatever went wrong wasn't his fault.

But she had to have the last word.

"Hey, it's your two million!"

"Look, I came back because I thought I could help Ruby," he answered.

"The arm bone connected to the shoulder bone," she sang. "And the Lord says you'll find the connections in the records, Town Hall, room 311."

"What!" He could no more see himself digging into files than fixing the bad plumbing. "C'mon, you're the reporter. The *Sentinel*, right? Gandee's weekly?"

"If it had cost *me* two million, I'd want to find out for myself."

"Foxx, you can be a real pain in the ass!"

She was actually amused by the insult. "Five years ago, Town Hall was renovated" she began. "They hadn't finished the job when the mayor was driving a new Caddie. How come a new Caddie? Well, would you believe he had everybody kicking back 15 percent on all contracts. Sheet rock, electric, painting, windows. He took a slice out of everything, right down to the toilet paper. It took me weeks of digging. I mean, I really put my butt on the line. I could see those headlines. I could see the Pulitzer Prize people sending faxes. I was a real reporter, by God! Of course, in the end, all I saw was zilch. You know, zilch, that good-for-damn nothing?"

"They didn't print it?"

"Hell, no. What I didn't know was who owned the *Sentinel* building. Why, it's the mayor! Not only does he own it, he charges the *Sentinel* hardly any rent! Can you beat that for smarts, Jack? If we ran the story, can you imagine how that rent would go soaring?"

"So you got screwed. Life ain't fair. Big deal."

"This time everybody got screwed, including you, Jack. And Cyrus got murdered. And Ruby is in jail."

It was a stunner, all right. He had no idea how to deal with anything like that. And he hated to hear about it—which made her a pain in the ass twice over. He even felt the need to defend his uncle.

"Well, Sam is the mayor, ain't he. He was elected, right?"

"Power, Jack. When you've got power you can do whatever you want," she said. "Anything. It doesn't have to make sense. Like in *Alice in Wonderland*, the Queen shouts 'Off with his head!' Ruby, poor Ruby. She knows what they can do to her. The face you saw was afraid of going mad."

He didn't know what to say. He couldn't even swallow. She was making the connections for him. From Town Hall to Black Jack Field to Ruby Coles, jamming them all down his throat.

As they drove back to the county jail, there was no further conversation.

When she pulled into the parking area behind the jail, stopped beside his Taurus, she simply reminded him.

"Gandee Town Hall, Jack, room 311."

"You bet," he said. More likely he'd be back at room 74 at the Plaza, screwing his brains out.

For all intents and purposes, Gandee was a one-tavern town—at least as far as whites were concerned. D.D.'s was owned and managed by Danny Duggin, son of Dave Duggin, whose father Donald had built the place when a young veteran of World War I. Three generations of D.D.s had kept everything as it was. Currently, a pair of neon beer signs lit up the plate glass window. The original D.D.'s sign hung over the door on a rusty iron bracket that remained unpainted. Everyone thought it was best left that way. As Danny said: "That sign has character!"

Jack had had his first glass of beer at this bar. He'd shot his first game of pool at D.D.'s table. He'd started, and ended, more Saturday nights here than anywhere else. The regulars included girlfriends, wives, fathers and mothers of all ages, and sometimes even babies. Occasionally, Gandee's elite came, like the mayor and his cronies, always welcome. Only people of color stayed away, and no one ever said they were conspicuous by their absence.

Fresh from a couple of hours in the pits with Foxx, this is where he wanted to be, and he walked in the smoky, jukebox-blaring, laughter-filled pub like a movie cowpoke after a long dry cattle drive. Who said you can't go home again?

First thing he saw was D.D.'s bald head shining under the colored neon. First thing he heard was a half dozen voices shouting greetings.

"It's *him*. Sonovabitch, it's *HIM!*"

"Hey, D.D., drinks on the house, right?"

"J.C., you still drink plain old Bud?"

Frank Fontarro looked as if he'd had so many over the years, D.D.'s might have gone dry. The fine lean body of a first rate shortstop was a tub of lard, the face puffy around watery eyes. Jack almost didn't recognize him.

"Hey, it's Double F!" he cried out, then reached to embrace him to conceal his embarrassment.

"Hey, Cuz. Lookin' good, man!" Jumbo cried out.

"Since when was I your cousin, Jumbo?"

"Since I got a base hit offa you."

"A practice game. A broken bat blooper in a practice game!"

"Ha! You remember!"

"It crushed me. 'The Hitless Wonder' and I gave you a base hit!"

"Man, I bat a thousand 'gainst you."

"Jumbo, I always thought you were the greatest."

"One beer for J.C. on me, D.D.," said Frank. "I figure guys like him, they don't carry no cash."

"All I got is in thousand dollar bills," Jack said.

"Hell, I can change that!" Jumbo offered, and pulled out three singles to prove it.

"Look, I'm buying him a beer. Say what you want 'bout me, say anything, but my kids are gonna remember that I bought the richest sonovabitchin' ballplayer in the world a goddam beer!"

Jack thought, they used to talk baseball in here. Baseball and girls, but mostly baseball. Now, because of him it was all about money.

At the bar, they crowded around him, the familiar and the vaguely familiar. He signaled to D.D. that *he* was buying, and there was no one there to question that. For fifty bucks, he would play the king for an hour, swept away by the bullshit of old times.

These were now his friends, all right. No autographs, no big-league-superstar pizzazz. It was as if he hadn't been away for more than a few weeks.

"Didja hear about Dougie's DWI? Ran his pickup through his mother-in-law's garden. Tell him, Dougie."

"I got the rhodos, missed the fuckin' zinnias."

"Best DWI I ever heard was Clarence Layton. Clarence was so shit-faced, he couldn't get the ignition key in, fell asleep with his head on the horn, and they locked him up, DWI just for *the noise!*"

"Clarence played good second base," Jack remembered.

"Good field, no hit," said Dougie.

"Story of my life," said Frank, who played excellent shortstop. Jack always liked Frank, a ball player who played for love.

"You saved that perfect game, Frank. Remember that play?"

"Sure do. Back-handed stab. Wish I had it on video."

"I umpired the bases that game," said D.D. "You couldn't believe it was in your glove."

"It was the base hits he couldn't believe most," Jack kidded him.

"Shit, I hit better than Cyrus—and I sure ran a lot faster."

"D.D., you were a lousy ump," said Dougie, imitating D.D.'s "out" call as if he were goosing a butterfly.

D.D. laughed with them. "I called 'em for over twenty years and never missed a one!" he boasted.

Jack shook his head. "I never met an ump who said anything different."

"Until Cyrus, I never met a nigger who couldn't run," said Dougie.

"One thing for sure: Cyrus couldn't run from his wife," offered Jumbo Deems, laughing at this own words.

"She must've been high."

"Crack high," said Dougie. "Clark Street is now called Crack Street."

Jumbo fixed on Jack. "They say you came back because of *Ruby?*" He made it sound almost beyond belief. "You're like the guy with his dick in a sack of cashews: you're fuckin' nuts, man!"

Big laughs at this mockery of the great one.

"Ol' fat Cyrus, full of holes. Shot-gunned dead by Ruby Coles. Poem by yours truly," said Jumbo.

"It's in the genes, you know what I mean?" Dougie said. "Ask Starger. That nigger cop knows all. Jesus, I wouldn't want that job."

"Take away his badge, he'd be cleanin' shithouses in the county hospital," said Frank.

"Cyrus, the plumber." Jumbo shook his head at the saying of it.

"Yeah, ask Gus Guida 'bout that!"

They took off on that one. Apparently, when the movie house had had a clogged toilet in the ladies' room, Gus hadn't been around to repair it so they got Cyrus. Next day, Gus was furious. He didn't want a nigger repairing what he did. So he went back and secretly switched the cold water pipe to hot. When a lady flushed, she let out a scream that stampeded the audience.

"Did Gus do the plumbing at Black Jack Field?" Jack wanted to know.

"Sure did," said Frank.

"Well, it stunk to high heaven," Jack snapped. His sudden anger surprised them. "I was there today."

"Yeah, with Foxx," said Jumbo. "Saw you go by."

"She been buggin' you, J.C.?" asked Dougie.

"Well, she give me some shit about how the paint company fire poisoned the ball field."

"I fought that sumbitchin' blaze," said volunteer fireman Frank. "Fierce, man. The worst!"

"Sure went up fast," Jumbo added. "Pfft! Like it was the way somebody wanted it to go!"

"Are you kiddin'?" Frank laughed. "It started in the northeast corner to catch the wind. Five gallon kerosene cans nobody ever saw before. I've seen arson, but that one beat all."

"Didn't they investigate?" asked Quentin. "I mean, I don't recall you testifying, Frank."

"How could I if I was in Arizona playing golf?"

"Didn't know you played the game."

Frank laughed. "I don't. I went for the tumbleweeds, always wanted to see tumbleweeds. But when I come back, that's when Foxx came at me asking about arson like I owned the match company."

"She's a garbage hunter, you know what I mean?" said Jumbo. "She digs so much garbage, she stinks of it."

Dougie laughed his way into a Foxx story. "Couple of months ago, she came snoopin' around the café. 'Unsanitary conditions', she said. Found a cigar butt in the stew. I said 'Hey, is it a Havana?' She walked through the kitchen looking for mouse turds in the corners."

"She find any?"

"A few here, a few there. Never was a kitchen without mouse turds. The little fuckers gotta live, you know."

"I didn't see nothing in the *Sentinel*," said Quentin.

Dougie grinned. "Hell, no, Quentin: we *advertise!*"

Jumbo laughed, repeating "A few here, a few there," and they all laughed some more.

"Man, there's so much shit going on in this town, you wouldn't know where it begins and where it ends," said Frank.

"Well, there's good shit and bad shit," offered Jumbo.

"All shit stinks," said Frank.

"That's fuckin' brilliant. You figure on putting your finger up Sam Manning's asshole to stop it?"

Frank laughed, but not happily.

"I got a five spot says you voted for him and you'll vote for him again this election," Jumbo went on. "Same as everybody."

"He ain't so terrible," Dougie said. "So you give a little, take a little. Hey, where's it any different?

"It's peaceful enough," Jumbo agreed. "Sam runs a tight ship, I'll give him that. You don't have to lock up and all."

"Just nigger crime," said Dougie.

"Don't bother me none," said Frank. "Your daddy gets my vote."

"He's one tough honcho, your daddy. When Sam put the badge on him, it was an okay day," Jumbo declared.

"John still whoppin' you 'cross his knee, J.C.?"

"The old 'Mark of the Five'" Jack laughed. "Made a man outa me."

"Shit, you ain't a man, you're a freak!"

Later, D.D. took him into his office for a chat, set a bottle of Jack Daniels on his desk.

"Good to see you, Jack."

They raised glasses then drank, neat.

"What's going on, Danny?"

"You came back, that's what."

Jack let it slide by. "I guess I got bored with all that money, my beautiful woman, everybody kissin' my ass, you know how it is."

"Tough life, all right."

"A couple of days in Gandee, clears the head. You get to appreciate your life more."

D.D. laughed at the thought. "Your head all cleared, Jack?"

D.D. was teasing him. Jack took his time about that, coming to grips with the confusions of the tavern scene. He was struggling with his ignorance, eager to rise above it. He was like a drunk trying to find his way out of a maze of mirrors.

"Things feel different here, D.D. Creepy, you know what I'm sayin'?"

"Different through your eyes, maybe. Not through mine."

"Well, this mess with Ruby Coles, Jesus!"

"That's just race. Race is in Gandee's genes. The colored came north after the Civil War, running from the South and the slave owners. There were jobs here but not nearly enough. Sooner or later, whites had to fight them off. Riots in East St. Louis, Cairo. Hey, the history of this town ain't no fairy tale. If I was colored, I'd find a way to get my ass out of here. My granddaddy used to tell stories that would make your head spin. Not only race hate but everything else, and I mean everything. Prohibition with stills-in-the-hills. Gangsters from Chicago, St. Louis. Whorehouses, gamblers, cops on the take. Race riots in the streets, one after another. What you gotta realize, Sam Manning is a product of that history. It's like he lived through six generations and knows how to survive. They call this town the asshole-of-the-world."

"Jesus. Does it have to be that way?"

"I don't know."

"Don't people object? Can't they vote him out?"

"They don't care enough to try. Oh, they're good guys, Jack. They're not saints, but they love their kids, they don't beat their wives, they pay their bills most of the time. Gandee may be shit-town but it's not their fault. Thieves pretty much run this country and Sam runs this town. I used to think something could be done. Even ran for mayor myself a few years back. What a joke! You came in here with your two-million-dollar ball park on national TV and all of a sudden Gandee seems like a big deal. But it ain't. It's the same bullshit town it always was. Whatever you might think you're gonna do here, forget it, Jack. It ain't gonna happen."

Jack always liked D.D. For one thing, he was a good umpire. He knew the rules. Called them as he saw them. With D.D. behind the plate, there was no nonsense in the game. Once he even went to the visitor's bench to stop their ragging of Cyrus. Everybody respected D.D.

"Sam came in here the other day," D.D. was saying. "He wanted volunteers to help clean up the square for Veteran's Day. 'We gotta clean the pigeon shit off the Colonel's statue!' he said. He's talkin' about the great Indian fighter who got rich selling rotgut whiskey to the Indians, then slaughtered them when they got drunk. Jesus, kill enough of them and they name a town after you! We've got the real American history in this town, Jack, only you don't read about it in school books.

"Did Sam get his volunteers?" It seemed important to know that.

D.D. laughed. "Your friend Frank told him there was no point to it, that the only way to stop them pigeons was to decoy them. Put up another statue of Sam himself, then they'd sure as hell shit all over that!"

Jack laughed, but his mind was lurking in dark corners.

"Been thinking about Cyrus, D.D. What do you supposed happened to him?"

"C'mon, Jack. What does it matter? Forget all that. You're the hero, kid. It's like one of us won a lottery, you know what I mean? Cyrus is dead. Shit happens, right? See that sign?

No Use Bitching, Nothing Matters.
No Use Pitching, No More Batters.

"That's the way it is, Jack. Like I said, nobody cares any more. Pretty soon everybody thinks maybe that's the way it's supposed to be."

"Mind if I use your phone, D.D.?"

D.D. shoved the phone across the desk. "Be my guest."

Jack dialed the Dodgers' club offices and asked for Adam LeBaron, groundskeeper. When he told them who was calling, Adam was promptly located on his car phone.

"I know, you want me to raise the mound another six inches," said Adam.

"I'll settle for three."

"How goes it, big man?"

"Adam, get this! A paint factory burns down. Everything burns to ashes. What happens to the soil? You know, the earth?"

"What happens? It's toxic. Dioxin. Paint is the worst."

"Dioxin? Don't the rains wash it away?"

"Shit, no. The poisons seep in. Water is a carrier."

"For how many years, Adam?"

"I dunno. Ten maybe twenty. You've got to keep testing it."

When he hung up, D.D. poured them both another shot.

"What was that all about?" D.D. asked.

"Just wanted to be sure."

"Okay, now you're sure?" D.D. was challenging him with his eyes.

"How could they get a permit to build on poisoned soil?" Jack asked.

D.D. was not happy with this.

"This is Gandee, that's how."

Jack had taken in more than he was prepared to absorb. Nor was there relief in one last shot of bourbon. When he looked up, he saw D.D. staring at him.

"Watch your ass, Jack!" D.D. said.

He was in Town Hall the following morning, probably the last place on earth he wanted to be. He had no wish to see the mayor this time. Not yet anyway. He walked up to the third floor, nervously approached room 311. "Records" read the sign on the door.

A middle-aged woman looked up from her computer, eyes squinting over glasses. She took her time before recognition, until finally convinced it was he, she said, "Young Cagle."

"Ms. Faye," he nodded, politely reading her name on the ID plate on her desk in front of her.

The purchase of the land for the Black Jack Field, he said. Might he see records of it?

"The deed," she corrected him.

She went to the appropriate file with the precision of a trained nurse in surgery. Inside of a minute she had a photocopy of the deed before him. The Gandee Commission (designated to create and construct the Black Jack Field) purchased twenty-six acres on Carson Road from the Realty Company of Helena Troy, Overton, Missouri, dated January 14, 1995. The price was $155,000. No mention of the Carson Paint Company.

"Is there anything else, Mr. Cagle?"

He looked up, grateful that she was not harassing him. She was, in fact, merely anticipating his needs.

"I thought this piece of land belonged to the Carson Paint Company," he said.

Without comment, she left him for a return trip to the files. Ms. Faye, it seemed, communicated exclusively in documents. As it turned out, Helena Troy had purchased the twenty-six-acre plot, this time from Galanter and O'Neill, a law firm in St. Louis representing the Carson Paint Company. The price was $32,000. It was dated December 2, 1994.

He picked up the other deed, held them both side by side. He reviewed the prices, struck by the enormous difference of $123,000. Then, the dates of purchase: from one hand to the other in less than six weeks!

("It's your two million," Foxx had said.)

Okay, okay. His tension was such, he warned himself to cool it. After all, this was not his sort of ball game. He knew enough about business to keep him aware of how little he knew about business. (Gordon, where are you?) He knew almost nothing about real estate. Show him a piece of paper with a law firm written on it, he would lay it on Gordon and run.

But from 32 grand to 155 grand in less than six weeks!

One other number suddenly became vital to round out the picture: the date that the Black Jack Field project originated. It was when Gordon and he had discussed it after last season. Gordon had already discussed it with the mayor. Jack had agreed, then left its implementation in Gordon's hands and went bear hunting in Canada with Corky.

Helena Troy bought the land from Carson Paint's lawyers in December.

Why did she suddenly buy twenty-six acres of dangerously toxic land that nobody had wanted? Who is Helena Troy with $123,000 of his two million in her pocket? What exactly did she know and when did she know it? And who, if anyone, set her up?

He was onto something, all right. He had barely stuck his toe in the water and here he was already treading in deep water.

Overton had always been a classier town than Gandee. There were no factory closings in Overton because there were no factories. No toxic smoldering ruins or race murders, just nice homes behind well-kept lawns and gardens. In Overton, they referred to Gandee as the dung heap of the county.

Helena Troy's real estate office was housed in a cozy white clapboard cottage with neatly trimmed shrubs. Her sign had a colorful floral design. On the blacktop driveway, a pale blue Cadillac of recent vintage had "HT 100" license plates.

He stopped his car across the street, wondering how to proceed. What exactly could he do? ("Ms. Troy, I was wondering how you managed to blah blah those twenty-six acres into a six figure gold mine."). No matter what he said or how he said it, he guessed that this was going to be a woman who would wrap him around a jeweled finger. Besides, she would have the home field advantage with her ground rules. He hadn't even scouted her.

She was a painted lady with too many hours in a beauty parlor, a forty-five-year-old pretending to be thirty. And not nearly as beautiful as she thought she was. He saw right off that her smile didn't work. His unexpected visit frightened her. She wasn't clever enough to handle it. He wasted no time taking her on, waving copies of the deed and the transfer in front of her eyes.

"How come, Miss Troy? How the hell did *this* happen?"

"What? I don't know what you mean."

"Why did you buy these twenty-six acres from the Carson Paint Company? What were you going to do with them? Sell lots on toxic soil?"

Too intimidated to reply, she immediately went fumbling in her purse for a cigarette.

"Or maybe somebody *told* you to buy them. Was that it?"

"Look, maybe you should take this up with Sam," she said.

Sam? he thought. Not "Mr. Manning." Not "the mayor." The intimacy seemed so obvious, it amazed him.

"Sam?" He stared at her, repeating the name as if to get a fix on the connection. "You're old friends? You and him?"

She had trouble lighting the cigarette, embarrassing herself while he kept attacking like a cop going after a confession.

"What in hell is this, lady? What've you got going with him?"

"I don't see where that's any of your affair!"

"It was my money! You walked off with $123,000 of my money!"

"So what? It's just doing business. It didn't hurt anyone."

"No? Last I heard, poison was bad for you."

"What poison?"

"Toxic poison from the paint company fire."

"Mr. Cagle, I don't know what you're talking about!"

She really didn't, he saw. He might have thrown a few more questions at her but saw no purpose in it. Only Sam Manning could give him the answers.

In the Taurus, however, his own motor was cooled by the prospect of such a confrontation. Could it really be that the mayor and this bimbo were fucking and stealing like a couple of scam artists in a TV movie? It was embarrassing. Jack felt like a kid who'd rather suffer a toothache than go to the dentist.

Returning to Gandee, he passed his old high school and slowed down, staring into the feeble afternoon sun hovering over the ball field. An off-season sun, he thought. Stare at the sky and think of the dreary months before you can play ball again. He remembered a late January morning when the sun had been a beautiful orange ball of fire. He'd hurried out of school at lunch time, had gone to the ball field hoping to see a patch of green peeking through the slush. He'd stood on the muddy pitcher's mound basking in the sweet feel of warm rays. And then, as if in some melding of souls, he'd seen Cyrus and Ruby. Ruby was shaking her head as she handed Cyrus a dollar.

"You two," she'd sighed.

"What?" Jack had asked.

"Hour ago, he bet you'd be standing here!"

Cyrus, laughing with his new dollar, had turned and slogged toward home plate and gone into his catcher's squat, pretending he wore a mitt, the whole bit. Jack, meanwhile, had toed the mound, his empty left hand behind his back, peering in for the sign.

"You cats scare me, you know," Ruby had said. "It's like you got somethin' so special. I ain't never gonna have any of it. What *is* it, Cyrus?"

"Baby, it's beautiful music. Ain't no reason to be scared. When that big white boy is on the hill, this fat-assed nigger makes him be the best!"

Jack accelerated as if to get free of the memory, then he saw his friend Frank's white logo "F.F. Construction" on a black pick-up truck in the school parking lot. Better a visit with an old friend than a brouhaha with his uncle.

"Hey, Frank, you still tryin' to pass algebra?"

"Algebra? Who'd he play for?"

They laughed at the greeting, but Frank was in no mood to enjoy it.

"The wind keeps blowin' and the shit keeps flowin'." He was seething like one about to put a fist through a window. "They called me to rebuild the bleachers. It's my high school, right? It's for the kids—some day, my own kids, so I'm ready to take short money. I quote low, real low. They say okay, go to work, but right off, the bastards want kickbacks. The school board! Then they tell me I gotta deal with

Wellington Lumber who sells me shit lumber at top prices. They fuck you around, Jack. Jesus!" Red-faced, eyes blazing, he kept going like a runaway freight train. "It was the same fuckin' thing with the Black Jack Field Commission." Frank had built the archway over the entrance. Sixteen foot span, the name in metal letters. He told Jack how he'd studied the specifications, estimated his cost at under five thousand dollars. For sixty-five hundred he figured he and his brother could do the job and make a decent profit. They paid him the sixty-five hundred, all right, but then hit him for special assessments, contributions to church charities, and Henry Ullman's son needed new kitchen cabinets. "It ends up, the fuckin' archway cost *me* over two hundred and fifty bucks!"

All through this tirade, Jack couldn't get over how much Frank had changed. Not only the extra weight but the puffy face and watery eyes.

"You look lousy, Frank."

"Can't imagine why," Frank scowled.

"Too many beers? What is it, Frank? Hey, you gotta take care of yourself."

"Get off it, J.C. You're still playin' ball. I'm here eating Gandee shit. If you was here, you'd be lookin' just like I do. You'd be a goddam dumbass sheriff's deputy making maybe ten bucks an hour, so don't get high and mighty, okay?"

"Yeah."

"Look, I ain't the only one. You seen Gus?"

Gus Guida was their first baseman in high school. Frank took Jack by the arm, leading him to the truck. "C'mon. He's at the diner."

Three old friends had coffee in a booth, but by the look of them you'd never know they'd been classmates. At twenty-eight Gus looked no better than Frank.

"We had a good ball team," Jack said. "Frank had the glove, you and me, Gus, we had the bats."

"Shit, man, you had the arm."

"And Cyrus had the mitt," Jack added.

"First nigger plumber I ever heard of," Gus said. "He bid for the Black Jack Field job. If I'd've been smart, I woulda let him get it."

"How come?" Jack wanted to know.

"Goddam job was for the birds. The whole thing was a rip off, right from the start. I give the Commission the specifications but *they* make the buy. That's Henry Ullman. What happens, I get a load of junk materials but get billed for top-of-the-line. Then they rake off 15 percent on all costs, but the vouchers read 100 percent. On top of that, I gotta kickback another 15 percent or else they gonna turn the job over to the nigger."

"I saw the job you did, Gus: It stinks," Jack said.

Gus laughed. "'Black Jackass Field' we called it. You get what you pay for."

"Not me, I didn't."

"You handed two million to that gang, like throwing a T-bone steak to a pack of wolves. What'd you expect, J.C.?"

"Sam's Scam," said Frank.

"Out of that two mill, pick a number. Sam musta walked off with maybe half a million!"

"Yeah, and Ullman bought himself a couple of new suits."

"Hey, Frank, you got any shit on you?" Gus asked.

"In the truck."

Jack was not happy with that either. "You guys do drugs?"

"Don't you? Quality shit, eh?" Gus asked.

"Not my style," Jack said.

Gus laughed. "Maybe if I made a hundred mill it wouldn't be mine neither."

"Drugs in Gandee?" Jack asked. "Since when?"

"Since Lorene, the Queen."

"The tavern on Clark Street?"

"Crack Street, you mean."

They remembered when the three of them sneaked cigarettes behind the diner, and Jack's father had caught them.

"Like we had just robbed a bank!" said Frank.

"He was like that," Jack said. "Crime is crime."

"He just don't see as good as he used to," said Gus.

"He sees what Sam wants him to see," added Frank.

Too much was coming at Jack too quickly.

"Not like the good old days," Gus said wistfully.

"Listen to him. Talks like an old man."

"Shit. We're in an off-season that don't never end," Gus sighed. "Man, you got it made, J.C.!"

They had nothing to say to each other after that.

Lorene's Tavern was Gandee's black D.D.'s, dominating the corner of Clark Street and County Route 61. A neon Budweiser sign hung over the plate glass window and a "Welcome" Coca-Cola sign over the front door. There was no mention of Lorene's on any sign, but no one ever thought of it as anything but.

As Jack walked in, a dozen or so black heads at the bar and pool table turned to see him. The place smelled as shabby as it looked—stale cigarette smoke embedded in tired gray walls, a residue of cheap whiskey and countless beers. Lorene was behind the bar, a full-figured dark brown woman in her fifties whose laughter turned sour when she saw who it was.

"We don't serve no white folk in here."

Jack put a hundred dollar bill on the bar. "You do now," he said.

Three stools down, a man laughed. Lorene glared to silence him.

"Whatcha want, J.C.?" she asked.

"Let's start with Heinekens, Lorene."

"You'll take a Bud. Don't have no fuckin' Heinekens!"

Jack shrugged as she set a bottle of Bud in front of him, no glass. She cashiered the hundred dollar bill without bringing change.

"What's going on, Lorene?" Jack posed the question as if he really expected some great all-inclusive answer.

Lorene barely acknowledged his existence. "Same old shit, J.C."

"It doesn't seem that way to me."

"That so? How's it seem to you?"

"Worse."

"Well, like they say, shit keeps happening."

"Like Cyrus getting killed, Lorene? Like Ruby in jail?"

"Maybe you askin' on the wrong side of town."

He was getting nowhere fast.

"Lorene, everybody knows somethin'."

"J.C., you been gone too long. That's what's going on."

"Well, I'm back, now ain't I?"

"Maybe you shoulda stayed away!"

Then she clammed up at the sound of a new arrival. It was the deputy, Lem Starger.

"Well, hi there, J.C. Thought that was your Taurus."

Jack nodded, shook hands.

"Everything all right?" Starger asked.

"Nothin' like a bottle of warm Bud," Jack grinned.

"What! Lorene, give him the best. Cold. On me."

"I already paid for the warm, Lem."

There were bar stool laughs at that one.

"Make it Heinekins, Lorene," Jack said.

She obliged him this time, and Jack nodded his appreciation to the deputy. "Hey, you gotta know the right people," he said.

Starger was smiling but his voice was grim. "You stayin' in town for a while, J.C.?"

Fishing, Jack knew. "Coupla days, maybe."

"Well, if there's anything I can do for you . . ."

Jack raised the Heinekins. "You just did."

Then he asked as casually as his voice would allow: "Which is Cyrus's house, Lem?"

"Third one down."

Jack finished his beer, taking his time about it. "Keep the change, Lorene," he said, then waved goodbye to Starger and left.

Third one down, Jack thought. He'd never been to Cyrus's and Cyrus had never been to his. As he approached the front door, he could hear children's voices inside. There was laughter and yelling, and then a man's voice hollering, obviously annoyed at what was happening.

He knocked, and soon enough, the door was opened by a half-naked five-year-old girl.

"Hi, there!" Jack smiled.

She ran off without a word, then Lukas came carrying another infant.

Like his sister Ruby, he was lean and wiry. His thin face looked as if he'd reached the last stages of frustration. Jack's appearance added to his scowl.

"Afternoon, Lukas," Jack tried hard to be cheerful.

"Wha'd'ya want, J.C.? I got a whole bunch of little problems here."

Five or six, Jack saw, wondering which were Cyrus and Ruby's.

"Isn't there a day care center down the block? Least, that's what the sign says."

Lukas grunted. "For the mayor's mommas only." He made it sound like an exclusive club.

"What?"

"You do for the mayor, the mayor does for you. Starts at prenatal, if you wanna know."

According to Sam, *everybody* loved the mayor on Clark Street.

Two little ones grabbed Lukas by the pant leg, a reminder of their presence.

"Wha'd'ya want, J.C.?"

He didn't know, did he? He just wanted to talk. This was going to be all wrong but he had to say something.

"Tell me about Ruby and Cyrus, Lukas. I mean, what happened?"

Lukas almost had to laugh. "Fuck you, J.C. I got these kiddies. See the kiddies, J.C.? Or am I dreamin' it? Ain't that the kiddies yellin', pullin' at my pants?"

It was like trying to scale a twenty-foot wall while others were shoving him back with a foot in his face. Little black children were laughing at him.

"Dammit, Lukas, what happened?"

Lukas glared at him.

"See this 'un?" The kid hanging onto his leg. "Joe Mape's kid. You know Joe? No? Well, he delivered for the UPS. Took him four years to get the job. Joe ain't around no more because he was a happy man. Yeah, I'm sayin' it right, man. He was deliverin' a package to the Reverend Morrow up on Sycamore Road, and he smiled at the reverend's old wife, did his funny little deliveryman jiggle. The reverend sees his wife laughin'. She's laughin' maybe the first time in twenty years. He don't like no nigger makin' 'er laugh. He calls UPS and tells 'em that Joe made lewd with his wife! He tells UPS to fire Joe or he's gonna sue! Oh, they fire him, all right. You want to hear the rest, J.C.? You want to hear how drunk Joe gets? Mad drunk. Mean drunk. One night he gets so shit-faced, he goes at Starger with a bottle! Joe Mapes is gone, J.C. He now lives in the state pen. Hey, little Joe, say hello to Mr. Cagle."

"'Lo Mista Cagle," said the small voice, just loud enough to hit like a fist in the stomach.

Jack felt his throat locking his need to swallow. He wasn't even surprised. It was like telling someone with cancer that he was going to die. Reverend Morrow had baptized him, preached countless sermons for all the Sundays of Jack's boyhood, ate his mother's cupcakes, but Jack was not surprised. There was nothing Lukas could tell him that surprised him.

"You hearin' me, J.C.? You get what I'm tellin' you?"

Jack nodded. What could he say?

"You wanna know what's goin' on in Gandee? This where Cyrus got killed. This where Ruby gets put in the can. This where your pig-shit uncle runs the world. You deaf dumb and blind, J.C., only you don't know it. You wanna know what's goin' on? Well, fuck you, motherfucker: *that's* what's goin' on!"

Outside, he saw two black kids smearing his windshield with dirty rags.

"Hey, thanks a lot kids!"

One had his hand out, palm up.

"Lorene says, this cost you ten dollars."

"For messin' me up?" He pointed to the windshield smear.

"For tellin' you to meet her at Omar's."

It took a moment for the words to sink in. He had nothing less than a hundred dollar bill. He put it in the open little hand.

"That ain't no ten!" But the other kid saw it for what it was.

"Where's Omar's?" Jack asked.

They took him around the corner and up an outdoor flight of stairs.

Omar's living room had the worn-out look of too many bad days. The carpet was spotted from too many spills. Toys had been hastily cornered behind the furniture.

Omar was a tall black around Jack's age, with a moustache, piercing eyes, and a single gold-plated earring.

They shook hands.

"Omar," Jack said. "How you doin'?"

"Not as good as you, man." Omar had a fast tongue, but the words were friendly enough.

So Jack went right at him, anticipating answers that set him tingling. "If I knew who killed Cyrus, I'd be doin' a whole lot better, Omar." Then he held his breath, waiting for the surprise he had come for.

He should have known better.

"If I knows that, I'd likely be as dead as him!" Omar said.

Lorene walked in. "There's maybe a thousand mother-fuckin' pigs in this town who coulda killed him but they lock up the one sure innocent."

So saying, she buried the entire question. What more could be said? Why had she brought him here? She glared at him, leaving him to wonder what new horror he had done to cause it.

"You come back because of Ruby Coles? All of a sudden you care so much 'bout Ruby Coles?" She was blanketing him with scorn. "You expect me to believe that?"

"Lorene, I don't give a shit what you believe!"

She laughed at him. "I seen this picture of you with Denzel, two big stars having a drink in movieland. Look at that, yeah! Jack Cagle ain't no redneck bigot, see? Why he's buying that colored man a drink! But how come I never seen no picture of you and Cyrus. You ever buy Cyrus a drink?"

It was as if God were a black woman punishing him for his sins. He hadn't come here for that. He wanted to find out what was going on.

"Lorene, I hear talk about drugs." He was challenging her now. "That Ruby did drugs."

Lorene looked at him like one who couldn't believe he'd said that.

"There ain't no drugs that could get Ruby to kill Cyrus or anyone else!"

"But you deal, don't you." Jack said.

"That what you come to see me about, J.C.? You a narc all of a sudden? Look out that window, what do you see? Ain't that Brother Starger sitting out there in his police car? Why don't you ask him? Ask him: *do Lorene deal the shit he keeps bringin' me?*"

"What!"

"You don't believe that J.C.? That shake up your big white ass? Why, it's your daddy's deputy dealing drugs! Ain't that the goddamndest thing you ever heard?"

She was taking him for a fast ride down slippery roads. He didn't know what to believe. She wouldn't let up on him, like a boxer who had pinned him against the ropes with a flurry of punches.

"What's happenin', J.C.? It's everybody playing the look-out-for-me game. The whole town's got the fever, the big *Mayor Me* spreading the disease. That's why Ruby's in jail. And that's why all us little *me*s gotta scramble around for whatever we can steal."

She had to laugh at her own words, then turned to Omar to share the pleasure of her wisdom.

"He listens, Omar, but he can't hear."

Omar laughed. "The man can pitch but he can't dance."

"Now ain't that somethin'!" Lorene concurred. "Hey, J.C., go tell Brother Starger I'm runnin' low!"

There were times when the home field advantage could really beat you.

J ack left Lorene's with their laughter ringing in his ears. Starger was still waiting, but Jack ignored him. This time, he was going straight to Town Hall to confront Sam. Nothing else could possibly mean a damn to him.

The trouble was that Jack had always liked his uncle. When Jack was a kid, Sam had always been there for him, gave him good presents at Christmas—a Swiss Army knife, gift certificates at the sporting goods store, another certificate at the movie house. Since those first years in Little League, Sam would come to games and cheer for him.

Everything was different now. When he drove down Webster Hill, he remembered Sam telling him how this very spot had been a turning point in his life. One rainy day Sam had been stopped at the base of the hill by a pool of water too deep to cross. Several cars were already stalled at the junction. Sam immediately borrowed a tow truck to haul cars across for twenty dollars apiece, the first time in his life he'd ever made three hundred dollars in a single day. He returned the next day to discover that an accumulation of leaves had clogged the drains. At the next rainfall, he'd added newspapers to create an instant flooding even deeper than the last one. One of his victims, this time, was a repeater named Carlos Sanguellan who owned an after-hours club outside of town. Recognizing a smart young hustler, Sanguellan had given him his business card, an invitation to a whole new way of life. With Sanguellan, Sam learned that being smart was not enough. You needed connections to get ahead, then more connections to stay ahead. All this led to Sam's election as the youngest mayor in Gandee's history. When

Jack's father returned from Vietnam and married Sam's sister, Sam saw to it that the war hero became the youngest sheriff.

Jack never forgot the bottom of Webster Hill; if Sam's success had begun with a gathering of fallen leaves, Jack's had begun with a broken bike at the Shell station.

When he walked into the mayor's office, Sam was ready for him.

"Hey, kid, did you hear about the guy with five dicks?" Sam's eyes were twinkling. "Yeah, his underwear fit him like a glove!"

Jack had come prepared to do battle, but Sam had him laughing in spite of himself. Even the sight of his 135-pound body in that giant leather chair was something of a joke, like a midget king on a throne, Jack thought.

"Sam, tell me about Helena Troy."

Sam's reaction was as light as a feather. No sudden pallor, no signs of shock. He smiled, just barely, enough to suggest he would enjoy every moment of this.

"She's the best, kid. Saved my life, in a way."

"Oh? What way is that?"

Sam took his time with this. Any mention of this woman was a matter deserving of reverence.

"Jack, my boy, from what I can guess you can raise a good stiff member, and with that classy woman of yours, you sure have a great place to put it. For your sake I hope it lasts forever." Sam shook his head, a lead-in to his own tale of disaster. "But sometimes it don't, kid. Fact of life. Your Aunt Abby is a beautiful and wonderful woman, the light of my life. But she's dead sexually. She had a hysterectomy and then, poof! Hormones? Glands? That was five years ago."

He spoke the words in normal tones. No bathos, no catch in the throat, no pleading for sympathy.

"Consider this, kid. I'm a normal man and I've got needs. I can tell you, it was like being half dead. Then I met the lady at a mayor's convention in St. Louis. She was somebody's secretary. First thing she said to me: 'Mr. Mayor, is something eating away at you?' Would you believe that? I mean, it was that obvious. . . . I tell you, kid, it was like being born again. I set her up in real estate. Everything then changed for the better. I loved Abby all the more. And I never regretted a moment of it."

It had all been reported with so much cool, Jack had to struggle to resume the attack.

"Sam, she made $123,000 profit buying and selling the site for the ball field."

The mayor's hand rose to correct him.

"She made no profit, kid. She was merely a front for getting the least expensive land we could buy. I turned that money into a special account I use to finance, among other things, a prenatal clinic and a day care center on Clark Street. That's what you have to do under economic conditions these days. In Gandee, you take from Peter to pay Paul."

"Is that legal?"

Sam smiled. "Must be. No one brought charges."

"She drives a new Caddie, Sam. From Jerry's, a lot like yours."

"Hey, a reward for services rendered."

Sam had an answer for everything.

"Gandee is suffering, kid. Some say it's dying. You must've had glimpses of it. Well, I'm bustin' my ass to keep it alive. Any way I can!"

Sam was not through yet, not by a long shot. Just as always, give him a shove and he keeps going and going and going.

"Let me tell you, we're not out of the jungle. You don't know what it's like, what's going on out there. How could you? These are bad times, kid. Small towns are becoming like endangered species. Too much poverty, too much crime, too much downright meanness. Biggest story in the country is race. Right here in Gandee, it's a fight to keep the lid on. I can tell you, kid, I'm no quitter. You wanna know why? Because I love this town. I love what I do to save it!"

"What about drugs, Sam?"

"Drugs. Where *ain't* there drugs? How can you stop them? We're a river town, kid. That stuff swims up the Mississippi!"

"They call Clark Street 'Crack Street,' Sam."

"Drugs and blacks go together like ham and eggs. Believe me, you gotta bend with that."

"Bend a little more, Sam: let Ruby Coles go free."

"Jack, you're a jewel. You always were. Maybe now even more. You're only a kid but you've got everything anyone could want for in this world. But best of all, I can see that you care about folks. God knows, that's rare these days."

"She didn't kill Cyrus. No way did she kill him."

Sam sighed, working for a way to handle this.

"What are we talking about here, kid? This is a complicated story, you know what I mean? Wheels within wheels. I'm saying it's likely to mess up your head, kid. I've seen enough of these things to know. You end up in a tangle, you don't get the answers you want."

"On Clark Street, they don't think she killed him, Sam." He liked the moderate tone of his voice. "Seems to me, you've got everything to gain by letting her go."

Sam smiled. "Sounds to me like you've had a busy afternoon, eh kid?"

"Let her go, Sam."

The mayor shook his head. "I can't do that, kid. This is a homicide. I couldn't do it even if I wanted to."

"C'mon, Sam, you arranged that plea bargain. You can just as easily get those dumb charges dropped."

The mayor swiveled in his big leather chair, halfway to the right, halfway back to the left, looking like a kid at a soda fountain.

"You're something, kid. A real piece of work, if you know what I mean. You let yourself get suckered. You bleed for them. I gotta admit, I'm like that myself. It shows a decent human being."

Jack felt his jaws tightening, anticipating the totality of Sam's rejection.

"You gotta learn to be careful where it takes you, kid. You gotta keep your eye on the prize. You're no ordinary fella. You're a big star. My God, there ain't no one in the whole damn world who wouldn't want to be in your shoes! So forget this nonsense. It don't add up to a wart on a pig's ass."

Jack cringed.

"Yeah, I know Sam, but—"

"Good! Then go. Bless you, kid. Go back where you belong." And he took one more look at his watch as if to punctuate the final words as he reached for his telephone.

Jack couldn't let him do it. Reaching across the desk, he held the phone to its cradle. At that instant, everything changed. Sam stared at him, stunned. Jack stared back. They were eyeball to eyeball.

"I'll make a deal with you, Sam: you get Ruby out of jail and I'll go."

"What deal? There's no deal. You're in no position to make a deal. You don't know what you're talking about. You've got no bullets in your gun. This is a question of executive power, pure and simple. What it means. How to use it. This is my ball park, not yours. You don't know shit about power."

"You're all wrong about Ruby!"

"Are you telling me how to run this office? I can't believe I'm hearing this! What got into you? I hear about you stickin' your nose here and there, makin' a big jerk of yourself. All of a sudden you think you're a rebel? Jack Cagle Jr. a rebel! Believe me, kid, I've known rebels and you're no rebel!"

"The deal, Sam. Everybody wins. Everybody."

The mayor's beady eyes glared like hot coals, his jaw thrust forward as if daring Jack to hit it.

"Just what the fuck do you think you're gonna do? Is that pea-brain of yours coming up with ideas? Like maybe you're gonna get some hotshot Jew lawyer to defend the poor little nigger widow? Or maybe one of those black TV lawyers?" Sam laughed at the scenario. "I got news for you: bad mistake. Big bucks trying to buy the criminal justice system. That's a real bad public image. You'll be a pariah in your little old hometown. The media will jump all over you. Ask your man Gordon. Ask your woman. You'll be a turncoat to your own father, the beloved war hero who made you a star!"

Jack could feel the juices draining out of him. Sam was too smart for him. Sam was grinning at him, flushed with his triumph, and his voice turned simpatico, oozing compassion.

"Go home, kid. Take it from your old Uncle Sam: go back to your woman. Forget all this bullshit."

Jack walked out like a pitcher leaving the mound after hanging one too many curve balls.

J ack's head was full of all the things he hadn't said. The kickback deals, the toxic field, the rip-offs of his two million dollars. An arsenal of weapons he hadn't fired. Even then he wondered if anything would have mattered, for Sam had been unbending. He was bullet proof. He would have laughed all the more.

He made it to the street half suspecting that Foxx would be there to mock his defeat. But when she wasn't, strangely enough he was disappointed. He was left to whip himself. It was time to quit. As Judith had said, he'd gotten it out of his system.

The neon-lit diner sign beckoned. He set his big body on a stool at the counter, and then there was a middle-aged woman with a pot of coffee and a sassy smile.

"Say, didn't you used to be Jack Cagle?"

Her name, Lila, was stitched over her shirt pocket. She gave good vibes at a moment when he needed them.

"How's it going, Lila?"

"You look like you don't want to hear," she said.

"I'll have some pie," he said, pointing to the shelves under the plastic dome.

"Take the cinnamon bun, Jack."

"I really don't much like—"

"What! What! I never heard of such a thing!" She faked genuine outrage.

"Hey, sorry."

"And you were always such a good kid."

"I know. I turned rotten."

"Take the bun, Jack, you'll be saved."

He had to laugh. "Okay. The bun."

She laid the bun on a dish beside his coffee. "Your troubles are over!"

"You're the best, Lila."

"You hittin' on me, Jack?"

"The way I feel, I'd whiff."

"How's the bun? Okay?"

"Not bad," he said.

"I baked them myself," she said. "Better than the factory junk. No big deal, but it's something. People like that, you know what I mean?"

She patted his hand and moved off to other customers.

When he tasted it again, he liked it more. And when he thought about it, he got her message. She was Lila-at-the-diner who baked cinnamon buns to make things better when most everyone else was making things worse. He let that linger in his thoughts, a feel-good moment that had caught him unawares. He watched her working the counter, a heavy-boned woman with a permanent twinkle in her large blue eyes and a never-say-never toss of her head. He could picture her being outrageous, like spilling soup in the mayor's lap.

He had to find a way to make a difference. Whatever it was, he couldn't quit on Ruby. Even if he just got her a lawyer. He would get her a hot shot, like Johnny Cochran. If nothing else, Sam's snide objections made it seem all the more appealing. It was an idea that began to feed on itself. In L.A. he'd have no problem making the right contacts. Someone who could turn the media on to a poor black widow being railroaded by a corrupt racist town. Why the hell not!

He drove back to the county jail to tell her this, wanting to see her light up at the prospects. He wanted to have her on his side, an acknowledgement that he was on hers. He would leave her with reason to hope.

At the jail, he was kept waiting for half an hour, then was told she refused to see him. There were no explanations. He took it to mean she'd simply had it with him. He was forced to retreat, another blow to his now fragile psyche. He walked out thinking he'd just about had it with himself.

And then there was Lem Starger wearing the smile of a satisfied man trying not to smile.

Jack couldn't wait to get at him.

"Starger, I'm fuckin' sick of you!"

"Just doin' my job, J.C."

"Oh? What job is that?"

"Seein' that nothing happens to you."

"*You're* happening to me. Nobody ever consider that?"

"Take it easy, J.C."

Starger didn't budge.

"You're wastin' your time here, J.C."

"Oh? How would you know that?"

"I know what's happening, that's how. Ruby's gonna stand trial, I promise you."

"I promise *you*, Starger: if she does, so will you!"

The threat took and the smile vanished. Not much of a victory but better than nothing. Jack went to the Taurus thinking that he was supposed to go home for dinner. He would call Judith on the way, turn the bad news of his failures into the good news of his return. She'd like that, he thought. He could go back to New York with something to look forward to.

In the car, he realized how tired he was, but there was comfort in the driver's seat. He had always liked cars. When he was a kid, he used to curl up in the back seat with a blanket. His mother once told him, the first word he ever spoke was "car," not "momma" or "dadda" but "car." He would stare out the car window and watch the world go by. Better than TV, even. When he'd bought a Corvette after getting his contract bonus, he'd driven off, living a beautiful dream. His first sex was in that Corvette, no easy matter for his big body to manipulate, but the baseball groupie in Yakima liked his car as much as she liked him.

He called Judith as he drove, pleading with the powers that controlled these things that she'd be in their suite. When she answered, she was as pleased as he was, immediately spilling over with her own news. She'd gone antiquing with her friend Barbara, an expert who ran the finest shop in Beverly Hills, so successfully, in fact, that she was considering expanding, and wanted Judith as a partner. Wasn't that exciting? Judith loved antiques. It was really quite an art form. There were even baseball antiques—

Because he was tired, he didn't react to a strange smell until it was too late. It took the cold barrel of a pistol under his right ear to bring it home to him. The phone was plucked from his hand even as she was speaking. A shadowy face in a ski mask appeared in the rear view mirror. Soft words instructed him to prepare to turn right at the next intersection.

"What do you want?" Jack asked. He was already reaching for his wallet. The gun in his ear was more terrifying than anything he had ever known.

"I've got five or six hundred bucks," he said. "Got a Rolex, must be worth ten or twelve grand—"

"Go by the next street. If you're a lucky motherfucker, you might end up still breathin'."

"What do you want?" he said again. "What in hell do you want!"

"Slow down, motherfucker, slow down."

Jack did as he was told, driving slowly as if to stall some inevitable disaster.

"Into that alley. That's right, slow and steady, man."

In front of the headlights, two men in ski masks were leaning against a car.

"You're done driving now, Black Jack. Get your ass out."

He was barely out when they jumped him. All three at once. Hard fists to his face and body. They came at him so savagely, it made no sense. Pumped full of instant adrenalin, he let loose with a wild cry of rage and tore into whoever was closest to him. Take one down with him. They had to be blacks getting revenge. Lukas's friends, maybe. Or Clark Street friends of Cyrus. Maybe even Ruby telling him to fuck off. This was race hate, pure bloody savage merciless race hate. He was sure of it, and he hated them all the more. He couldn't see their faces, but he didn't have to. He was afraid they were going to kill him. He cried out a hatred of his own: "You sonsovbitches! You fucks!" and tore into them like a wild man, kicking, throwing wild punches. He had never been a street fighter. He'd never had to be. He was fighting with nothing but rage. If he was going to die, he would die fighting. But he was helpless, blinded by the headlights, swinging at silhouettes. They came at him from all side, pounded his ribs, his face. Fists in his face. He'd never been hit so hard, so repeatedly. Bodies rolled on the damp ground, and they grabbed him from behind, pinning his arms, and the third went to work on him, kicking him hard in his stomach, his ribs, then they punched his head until he lay like a fighter being counted out. For a while, he was aware of dirt under his face as he tried to breathe, and then, at last, there was nothing.

His first awareness was of Judith's perfume. Even before he could open his eyes, he knew she was there. He was smothered in a dense drugged fog, but he could relate to that fragrance.

His moan brought her kiss.

"You are Black Jack Cagle and I am the Angel of Love," she said into his ear.

He opened his eyes and there she was. In a hospital room. He could smell that too. The room was in shadows from a single bedside lamp. His body lay so heavily sedated, he could barely feel its existence. He moved to touch her but couldn't make it. She took his hand in hers, kissed it. He remembered fists to his face, his body. He could never forget those fists, like explosions in his brain.

"Where am I?" he asked.

"St. Louis Barnes Hospital." She explained the rest of it. "They found you yesterday morning in the back seat of your car. You've been out of it, baby. And I can tell you, the whole world has been put on hold."

He remembered the guy in his car, the gun to his ear. He'd been talking to her on the phone. It pleased him to remember.

"Yeah. Must've been twenty of them," he tried to make jokes. "Came at me with clubs, chains, attack dogs."

"Dogs! That's not fair."

"I was always nice to dogs."

"Well, you're going to be fine, baby."

"Good as new," he agreed but he could hardly keep his eyes open. His last thought was that he was happy to be alive.

When he awoke again, Judith was still there, curled up in the chair by the window.

"You slept like a baby," she said.

It was dark outside. Last he remembered, it was day.

"What's happening?"

"Outside that door, they're all there. I mean, lots of them. I'm just the Designated Angel."

He grinned at that. She came to his bedside, took his hand. It felt warm in hers.

"I'm supposed to call the doc," she said.

"The doc? What do I need a doc for?" he mumbled. "I'm perfectly all right."

"Sure, but can you get it up?"

He considered that.

"Call the doc," he sighed.

The doctor reported fractured ribs, multiple bruises, no internal injuries. All in all, he'd be all right quickly enough. He advised Jack that everything this hospital had done had been supervised by specialists from his ball club.

"Consider yourself a lucky man, Mr. Cagle."

"Luckiest man in the world, Doc."

The doctor smiled. "Well, you need rest. That's all."

He nodded. Rest. How could he not rest when he could hardly keep his eyes open.

He was fading off to sleep again, this time blessed by the official news of his survival.

Judith kissed him again. He could barely feel it.

"I'll be here," she said, then left with the doctor. Jack spent the next six hours back in oblivion.

He felt a lot better when he came out of it. When they let the media in, he could almost enjoy it. TV cameras angled through IV tubes for a close-up of his battered face, reporters with the usual ludicrous questions. Even Sam Manning, the greatest of all take-charge guys.

"Tell 'em what happened to the other guy, kid?" Sam was a bundle of good cheer.

"One little guy, no more 'n 120 pounds," Jack said. "But I just couldn't handle him. It was like he had twelve fists!"

There was laughter, cameras flashed.

"Can you tell us what they got?"

"I had five, six hundred."

"Jewelry? A watch?"

"Yeah, a Rolex."

"How'd it happen, Jack?"

He told them the simple story.

"Damn muggers!" Sam hissed.

"Were they black?" a reporter asked.

"Yeah."

"We'll get 'em," Sam snapped. "No question."

Sure, Jack thought. No question about it. It crossed his mind that the media were here to see him before the police. Sam always had his priorities straight.

Then he saw his father and mother at the door. Emma came to his bedside, kissed his cheek and broke into tears.

"It's okay, Mom."

"Emma, please." John took her arm.

"Gordon called," his father said. "Three, four times."

"And maybe a thousand others," added Emma.

"Hate to bother you 'bout this, Son." He was John, the sheriff, now. "But can you give us anything we can use? Any ID?"

Jack shook his head. "They wore masks, Dad. There were three guys." Then, "Why would they want to hammer me like that? I mean, the guy in the car had a gun."

"It's all race hate, kid." Sam said. "It ain't enough to take your money, they gotta hurt you, too."

"I guess."

"Maybe you'll remember something that'll help. Try. Like something in the tone of voice."

Jack couldn't help him. Everything was a blur.

"I'm still groggy."

They left him with Judith. She sat by the bed, all smiles. She was there for him, all right. He had an eerie feeling that she had never been so happy. She would take him back with her and turn the torment of the mugging into a love fest. She would be in control now and there would be no more Gandees. She leaned over and kissed him gently, and almost immediately, he went back to sleep.

He awoke in pain as a fist crashed into his rib cage, a dream so intense that he cried out. Moments later, a light came on and a nurse appeared.

"A dream," he explained.

"It happens a lot," she sympathized. Was there anything he wanted? A cold drink maybe?

"A Coke would be fine," he said.

Injuries tended to hurt more a day or two later. Any athlete knew that. It wasn't the pain that bothered him, knowing he would recover, it was the rest of it, the confusing compounding of horrors that had brought him here. He could feel the thugs working on his rib cage. Brutal stuff, and sly as a fox. He didn't want to think about it, afraid of where his thoughts might lead him. They didn't want his Rolex as much as they wanted to punish him. Whatever it was or it wasn't, he began to suffer his anger.

And then there was Gordon on the phone.

"I'll tell you somethin' Jack: it was super on TV. Black Jack as victim! I clinched the Jap deal at *five* million!"

Take a beating and Gordon will turn it into a victory.

"Glad to hear."

"Your medical report is fine. I want you to rest in L.A. for two days. Judith says she'll take care of everything. I'll meet you there on Thursday, then on to Tokyo."

"Thursday's fine."

"I've prepared a statement you should make to the media. I'll fax it to you. Deliver it at the press conference when you leave the hospital. You must denounce racism, even though you were mugged by blacks. Give it all you got, Jack."

"Sure thing."

Then there was a moment when the phone went awkwardly silent, for Gordon had never allowed that to happen.

"What's going on there, Jack?"

There was fear in that voice—as if he'd been taken over by an alien force. It was Gordon without his pockets on.

"Beats me," he said, then realized the double meaning of his words. "A joke, Gordon."

"Not funny."

"No big deal. It was like bumpin' into a door."

"Jack, you're not lookin' where you're goin'. Are you forgetting something, Jack?"

The repeated sound of his name bothered him. Gordon was referring to money, of course, his perpetual emotion. Jack had to admit that. He'd made "a wrong turn up Green Street," to paraphrase Cyrus, and he was getting his wrist slapped because of it. For it all, that too was a joke because now it seemed he would end up making more money because of it.

But Gordon was like a boulder rolling down a mountain. "Some of you guys get too cocky for your own good. They get crazy ideas about wanting to 'be themselves,' as if they knew what that meant. Are you readin' me, kid? The truth is, you big deal jocks haven't the foggiest! You've been pampered since childhood; you wouldn't know how to make a flight reservation but you think you can take on the world."

"Okay, Gordon—"

"Hear this, kid, a fable I heard when I was a boy. It's about this rabbit, dead tired, cold, starving, it collapses in a field, it's gonna die. But then a cow comes along and dumps a load of shit on him. By God, the rabbit gets warmed and nourished by it, shakes himself off and climbs back out into the open, happy to be alive. Except, a hungry fox sees him and gobbles him up. Do you get the message, kid?"

"What, Gordon?

"When you're warm and safe in a pile of shit, *don't move!*"

"Okay, I was dumb."

If Gordon was finally pacified, it was mostly because of his own words. "Yeah, all right, I'll catch up with you in L.A."

"Yeah."

"Then we go to Japan."

"Yeah, fine."

"You're gonna be okay, kid."

"Hey, you bet."

"You're lucky. Remember that. You've got Judith and you've got me."

Plus a fairly decent left arm—but he made no mention of that.

He called Corky, looking for a laugh, whatever the damage to his ribs.

"Roomie, if they've got mirrors in your room, bust 'em!"

"That bad, eh?"

"My kid saw your face on TV, he cried out, 'Uncle Roomie musta had a fight with Batman!'"

If he didn't want to laugh, he should never have called him.

"One thing I know: I'm hurting."

"Yeah, but why? I can hear what's happenin' there. I don't hear nothin' 'bout why."

Jack grunted into the phone. It was like asking a pitcher why he had walked the last hitter. Why?

"Yeah. What can I tell my kid so he won't think you're the second biggest jerk in the U.S.A.?"

"Who's the first?"

"He says me 'cause I roomed with you."

"You? Tell him not to worry."

"That's it? Don't worry?"

"Yeah, that's it."

"Roomie, you just made numero uno."

Jack tried not to laugh.

"Remember the Alamo!" cried out Corky.

The Alamo. Not the fort but a Texas tavern and "a night that will live in infamy," Corky had called it. The two of them had stopped for a few beers after a game. A handful of redneck dudes in big Texas Stetsons and spangled boots thought they'd have some fun with the celebrated pitcher and his black friend. Blessed with the home field advantage, one hate-word piled on another, and eventually fists began to fly. Almost immediately, the police moved in. This was big media stuff. The two visitors from L.A. ended up in jail for disturbing the peace. This was where Corky, bruised but indomitable, lying on his bunk, had delivered his sermon on American racism.

"I have a dream," he'd announced in stentorian tones. "I have a dream that someday professional baseball will be completely segregated. No black man will play on the same team or in the same league as a white man. National League, all black. American, white. Managers, coaches, trainers, front offices, the whole damned set-up. Every game will be interleague. Stadiums will be divided. Odd number section down the right field line, only white spectators. Even numbers down the left field line, all blacks. Umpires, the racial coloring of the home team park. Likewise the choice of food, the vendors, the between-innings music. All games then, will be a racial clash. I have a dream, Roomie, of high-flying spikes, of pitchers decking hitters, of body-crashing drama at home plate, of violence and rumors of violence. I have a dream of great rivalries spurred by racial pride. Colossal ball games that would inspire ballplayers beyond fat pay checks. Baseball will become the heart and soul of racist America, bringing in crowds beyond the greediest club owner's dream. The World Series, then, would be a modern reprise of the Civil War itself. I have a dream, Roomie, where the bullshit hypocrisy of America's quest for racial amity will once and for all be abandoned!"

"It won't work," Jack had said.

"Why not?"

"You guys would win."

"Hey, you're wrong. Whites lose one World Series, then everything would change. Whites would teach baseball in the schools, in the churches, in the shopping malls. There'd be a dozen times the number of Little White Leagues financed by white communities throughout the nation. White pride, white power, white hope would prevail. In no time, there'd be a new Babe Ruth, a new Joe DiMaggio, a new Sandy Koufax. It's what happened to American science when we saw that Sputnik in the sky. By God, it was a time when you couldn't buy a slide rule for love or money!"

"That's some dream," Jack said.

Jack also remembered how the media had had a field day over the incident, primarily because of one picture of Black Jack with what looked like a vicious headlock on a man whose Texas Stetson was being crushed in the midst of it. The man subsequently got a thousand dollars for that hat, and Black Jack became known as double the terror, as much off the field as on.

Corky wasn't through yet.

"Hey, Roomie, you missed your big chance with that 'I'm-not-a-racist' bullshit. Ain't you Black Jack Cagle, the meanest sonovabitch who ever stepped on the mound? Man, you should've savaged those black bastards. You should've said you'd find them three motherfuckers and nail them to the wall! Nobody, I mean, nobody, would say you were anything but a hero!"

"Corky, you are one sorry bad-assed black man."

"Shit, man. Who else have you got to keep you on line?"

"I hear you, man."

"Hey, remember the Alamo!"

Jack hung up laughing, for all was now right with his world. Corky was really not crazy at all. Sometimes being wild made more sense than being sensible. How else could it be after what Jack had been through? The mugging had turned everything around. He could rejoice in his wounds like a soldier wounded in battle, for the war was over for him. He could go home as a hero. Even his father seemed pleased with him. The mugging made his shit-kicking return to Gandee into a triumph. If he'd failed to help Ruby, no one could say he hadn't suffered for the trying.

He could leave now.

Two days later, Judith arranged for a limo to take them to the airport. She also had a wheelchair ready for him, which, to Jack, was a hoot. She pushed him to the starting gate, cornered the chair as far from the others as possible. She bought him magazines, *Sports Illustrated, People, Playboy,* and laid them on his lap, then went happily off to take care of tickets, boarding passes, baggage, make a few last minute phone calls, do her pre-flight ablutions.

So here he was maybe fifteen minutes from returning to the real world of his pleasures. He had only to look at *People Magazine* to see what the world thought of him for there was the battered face on a full page. "Black (and Blue) Jack" they called him.

He went from *People* to *Sports Illustrated* for other pictures and other words when he heard her sad sympathetic sigh.

"Oh my, you really *are* a mess, aren't you?"

Foxx.

"It only hurts when I laugh," he said.

"It's terrible!"

"I'll live." Then, to clear the air: "Just get me on that plane."

She seemed not to hear him.

"You came, you saw, you got conquered."

"The word is mugged, Foxx."

"Yes, but more than yes."

"They took what they came for, then reminded me what color I was."

"They were sending you a message, Jack. *Somebody paid them to deliver it!*"

"What? What message?"

"Get out of town!"

"C'mon, Foxx." He wasn't buying any of this.

"This *is* the departure gate, isn't it?"

She could be sarcastic without sounding superior. He could have argued that he was going to leave anyway, but he chose to ignore her.

"There's some unfinished business, Jack."

"Not mine, there ain't."

He heard the sound of his callousness, sensing he was losing control. He should never have allowed it to begin with. Where was Judith anyway? On a telephone? In front of a mirror? Or was she having fun flirting with the ticket agent?

"Ruby." Foxx's voice suddenly broke. He saw her lips moving but nothing came out. She swallowed hard, then began again, tiny tear drops forming in the corners of her eyes.

"She had an episode last night."

"A what?"

"She flipped out, yelling, screaming that she wanted to die. They got her to the hospital," she went on.

This was what she had come to tell him, wasn't it. She had to tie up all the loose ends. He was about to leave, mugging or no mugging, but she had to deliver one last killer goodbye. It wasn't his fault, was it? He couldn't help what had happened. He had tried to help her, hadn't he? What did Foxx want of him? The closeness of everything crowded in on him, and he remembered Ruby's depression when he saw her last. At the time, however, he had considered only his own. Foxx never stopped hitting on these connections. When you looked at Foxx, you caught a whiff of inevitable doom.

Then she assembled her things, picked up her bag, suddenly struggling under its weight.

"What they say about you," she shook her head at the magazines in his lap. "Don't think you're a hero, Jack. You didn't make it happen. You want to know why? You really didn't care. That's the way you live. You're a super jock celebrity with a money manager for a guru and a flashy lady for a soul. That's the way you think it's supposed to be."

She looked at him through those big sad eyes and spoke her last words: "You know something, Jack? You don't even know that you don't know."

And then she was gone.

His heart was pounding in a fractured rib cage. He had no wish to think. Whatever she had said had to be vaporized before it penetrated his brain. He needed Judith. He turned to look for her but all he could see were the dozens of waiting passengers around him, glancing his way, the usual celebrity-clinging bullshit looks.

Suddenly, the goddam wheelchair was insulting his pride. He had to get out of that chair to liberate himself. He took a deep breath, defying the pain that stabbed his ribs, then slowly let out air as he grabbed the arms, pushing himself to his feet. Beyond him, he heard a collective gasp like a group in shock, then a sigh of relief as he stood erect. His legs were so unstable, he began to totter, step by step, toward the window. This brought on a slowly gathering cheer, then a rising burst of applause, then unbelievable gales of laughter. It was a massive sound so alien to an airport, so jarring to his mood, it was seconds before he understood what had occurred: they were witness to a miracle! The curing of a cripple! This was Lourdes in the St. Louis airport! When he turned to them, he saw over a hundred people with beaming faces, clapping, waving, laughing, cheering. Because of what he had just done, they had lived a marvelous joke on themselves and wanted to share it. He saw their affection, just when he needed it. He smiled and waved. He couldn't help himself. Black Jack smiled! He laughed with their laughter. For the first time in his life he laughed with a hundred strangers.

He felt giddy. He had turned tail on one morbid reality and grabbed at a joyous one. His giddiness delighted him for he saw the scene as a summing up. This was the way the farce had to end.

And there was Judith, standing by the chair, laughing with the others, having seen enough to share in the victory. He returned to the chair feeling as joyous as he was miserable when he'd left it. It was an invitation to what became an autograph party. Starting with a six-year-old boy with a crayon and a coloring book, he scratched his name on everything from the inside of a match book to a Bible opened to the last chapter of Genesis. He actually enjoyed doing it and everyone was grateful. Besides, he knew it would never happen again. Nothing like today would ever happen again.

"Flight 616 to Los Angeles now boarding at gate 4."

Whereupon Judith finally shooed them away.

"Leave you alone for a minute and you break all the rules," she said.

"I needed the exercise," he quipped. "Did you get any chewing gum?"

She leaned over the wheelchair to kiss him, passing a wad of gum from mouth to mouth.

"I know a guy who got AIDS that way," he said.

"Not with Dentyne. Says so right there on the wrapper."

"Clap, then."

"Wrong. Haven't you heard? You get clap on a toilet seat."

"We better not do it there, then," he said.

She was getting her things together before boarding. "You're funny," she said.

Nobody had ever said *that* to him before.

For Jack, first class seats meant that boarding passengers coming down the aisle would stare at him. On this day, however, he didn't mind, and he met their laughing eyes from his window seat. Judith fussed with the cosmetics in her handbag, prattling on about how hospital smells clung to you for days, how there ought to be a special deodorizer sprayed on you when you left. Then she segued into the drabness of nurses uniforms, especially those ugly shoes for the way they insulted a woman's legs. She could never become a nurse if she had to wear those shoes.

A young voice called to him: "Get well, Black Jack!" and Jack waved at a kid with his father, conscious of a strange reversal of roles, for he had met Judith in that L.A. hospital while telling a battered kid to do exactly the same thing.

Then, as Judith was filing her nails, she mentioned that "baggy redheaded reporter (ugh!)" who had glared at her in the airport "like maybe I had two noses or something too gruesome for words!" For Jack, there was something ominous about this sudden intrusion. How could he get free of her? "Those glasses she wears! She doesn't care *what* she looks like!" The glasses triggered a crazy memory from the school yard where he and his friends were laughing and cheering at a fight between a white girl and a black girl until Foxx came out of nowhere to break it up like a boxing referee trying to separate a clinch, and her glasses flew off in the skirmish. When she put her glasses back on, she glared at them all in astonishment. How he had hated that look! It was as if he had started the fight. No one had ever looked at him like that before. Not even his father.

He turned to the window to watch the pre-flight loading chores on the tarmac, eager to get off the ground, annoyed at the fuel trucks and baggage carts and catering vans still at work. They were already ten minutes past flight time and his impatience began to feed on itself. Only by being airborne could he feel liberated. Only by changing his geography could he find relief. He told himself that in a few hours they'd be in L.A., where they'd be performing the most therapeutic act in all of human history.

But Judith was still in her foxhole.

"She's so *creepy!*"

He'd never heard her use that word. It was as if she'd been saving it for Foxx. All wrong, he thought. Creepy was a spider crawling up your leg. Foxx was anything but.

"She's not creepy, Judith," he said while looking out the window, barely audible even to himself.

"You're mumbling, Jack."

"Look! I'd just as soon not talk about her!"

She quickly caught his drift. To Judith, his sudden rancor suggested intriguing complications she found irresistible. She even stopped her nail filing to take him on.

"My, my, what plays here, Jack? Don't tell me you had something going with *her!*"

The way she said "her," he could picture her face writhing in disgust. He didn't comment, hoping she'd let it pass. His silence, however, convinced her she was pushing the right buttons.

"You did, didn't you!" She couldn't have enjoyed this more. "What was it like to fuck a sow, Jack? Did she squeal?"

He wished this bullshit would go away. She was so far off base, it amazed him.

Compared with Foxx, Judith seemed childlike. Foxx had *really* hurt him, especially at the departure gate.

("You don't even know that you don't know!")

Twice cursed by his stupidity. Not only blind but deaf. Not only dumb but uncaring.

("That's how you live. You think that's the way it's supposed to be!")

She was in tears when she'd said these things. Not just for Ruby but for him, too. She was crying because he had failed, exactly as she'd expected him to. She was crying for everyone.

("The arm bone connected to the shoulder bone.")

He felt sweat forming on his back, the stinging of nerve endings on the surface of his flesh. Suddenly he had trouble breathing as his heart pounded against his ribs. He rubbed clammy hands against his thighs, closed his eyes to forestall dizziness, pressed his forehead against the plexiglass.

Judith was still chuckling away, a master of mockery.

"Hey, I understand, Jack. I mean, I used to dream of fucking King Kong!"

He could make no sense of her words. Her voice sounded so distant, it was like something from another world. When he finally turned to look at her, her laughter frightened him. He was sweating profusely now. He thought that this would not be happening if they were airborne. Delays on the ground always made him uneasy. Suddenly, he had to get off the plane. When he looked at the cabin door, it was still open, but the flight attendant was standing beside it, hands on the lever. He unclasped his safety belt and got to his feet. There was nothing in his life more vital than getting to that cabin door.

"What are you doing, Jack?" Judith cried out.

"I've got to go!"

"Why? What's wrong!"

"Come on, Judith!"

He was in the aisle, tugging painfully for his bag in the overhead rack.

"What is this! Where are you going?"

"C'mon! C'mon!"

"Are you crazy?"

"I've got to, I've got to!"

He shouted at the flight attendant to hold the door. He had his bag beside him, reached up for hers.

"Judith! C'mon!"

"Don't you dare leave, Jack. I don't believe this! Sit down, Jack. *Sit down!*" She kept shouting at him as he moved off. "You've gone mad, Jack. What are you doing! I don't believe this. Jack!"

The flight attendant held the door for him, and he left the plane like one fleeing a burning building.

15

The wheelchair was still in the breezeway; with nowhere else to go, Jack sat again, half expecting Judith to change her mind. At first, he didn't really believe he had done this, for nothing in his life had prepared him for it. It occurred to him that he actually might have gone mad, a momentary episode, maybe. Could it be that he was suffering some weird side effects from his medication? Or some stress reaction to the savagery of the beating? Sitting in that wheelchair, he didn't know who he was, he didn't even feel like himself, it was too crazy to be real. Why was there no pain? He had suddenly gone numb, another indication that, for the first time in his adult life, he was totally alone. Not only alone but adrift. The great Black Jack Cagle had painted himself into a frigid corner where he sat shivering like a lost dog, cradling his travel bag as though it were all he had left in the world.

"Oh, man!" His sigh was a whisper that concealed his desperation. He hadn't the slightest idea of what he was going to do.

From out of nowhere, a small black airline employee stepped in front of him. "Alvin Agar" read the ID tag pinned to his jacket. Large eyeglasses dominated his narrow face. He stood there, hands on hips, smiling like a friendly owl.

"What's happenin', Black Jack?" His high pitched voice extended the classic black man's greeting. "You need some help?"

Jack had to laugh just looking at him. Alvin seemed resigned to his funny face as if, long ago, he had learned that there was nothing he could do about it.

Jack liked him immediately.

"Need all the help I can get, Alvin," he said, a confession that satisfied his soul.

"Man, it's my mission in life to help my fellow man—especially if he got a hundred million dollars."

Jack laughed. "You wouldn't help me if I was poor?"

"Hey, it's you, Black Jack. Be real! Ain't you heard? It's money makes the wheels go 'round."

"Well, like they say, it can't buy happiness."

"No? *No?*" Alvin was shocked. "Man, you just ain't spending it right! You got no right to be unhappy. When you got the dough, you run the show!"

Jack saw no reason to stop him.

"I *dream* of it! I want that crisp new smell like it's fresh from the mint, I want to rub it on me. I want to fuck on it." Then he moved behind the chair and pushed Jack up the breezeway.

"Where to?" He sounded so much like a cab driver, Jack shook his head, confused by the simplicity of the question and the complexity of the answer.

"Take me to your leader, Alvin."

The chair stopped on a dime. "Man, you askin' me to tell you where you wanna go when you don't know yourself? No way!"

Anywhere but here, Jack thought. "Put it in cruise control, Alvin. Let's see where it takes us."

"That redhead do a number on your head, man?"

"What redhead is that?" Jack asked, needing a moment to adjust.

"She go out cryin', you come out sighin'. *That* redhead."

"You've got big eyes, Alvin."

"Big ears, too. That redhead was smart."

"Yeah? How smart?"

"Smart enough to know you got fucked over by pros. Them guys were *paid*, man."

"What? How do you know that?"

"Shoot pool at Manny's, you hear all kinds of shit."

"Tell me about it, Alvin."

Alvin smiled. "I push you for money, I tell you for money."

Jack let it roll around in his head. Could he believe this little man? Then, too, why not? He even liked the way Alvin was hitting him for money. What was more honest than a man working for money?

"I'm looking at five beautiful Gs, big man."

"My credit good?"

"As good as it gets."

"Push me to Manny's then."

Alvin had to laugh again. "Money makes the wheels go 'round."

Jack sat in Alvin's Chevy with his knees high against his chest, but he didn't care. Because of Alvin, he was doing something that justified his getting off that plane. He had a tour guide with a definite plan, a no-bullshit, money-hungry black man who was going to teach him how to spend his money and buy happiness.

"Lemme tell you 'bout a Christmas when I was a kid. We got no daddy. He run off because he fucked up his life. My momma is pissed 'cause she's gotta scrub floors and shit like that. My sister is gloom and doom and won't go to a Christmas party cause she got no pretty clothes. Me, I'm fifteen, I got eighteen puny bucks from baggin' at the market. So okay, I get in a crap game, hot roll it up to two-sixty. Now that's money! I give my sister seventy-five to get herself pretty. I give my momma a hundred and a dozen roses. And I buy me a new baseball glove. Happiness, man. I bought us Christmas, and you never seen so much classy love."

"You're my man, Alvin."

"You bet your ass, big man."

Manny's Pool Parlor was neon lit, a few miles from the airport.

"Wait here," Alvin said. "You walk in with me, you'll scare their dicks off."

Jack nodded. Alvin was always one step ahead of him. Alvin made him think of Gordon, but Alvin was smarter. With Alvin, every situation was different. With Gordon, every situation was the same.

After ten minutes, there was Alvin gesturing to him. He said nothing as they climbed to the second floor where he led Jack to a table in the rear. He was Black Jack, as recognizable as the U.S. president, and heads turned to watch them.

They stopped at a pool table where two large black men stood waiting. No way he could recognize them.

"This's Owen, man."

Owen laughed, "We already met."

"Mace," said the other, not quite as big as Owen.

For privacy, Alvin led them to a booth at the side of the bar where they sat with a pitcher of beer.

"So, okay, talk," Alvin said to Owen.

"You're looking to pay for the guys who whacked you?" he asked Jack.

"Yeah."

"Okay, here's two of us."

"How do I know that?" Jack asked.

"I got $520 from your black wallet," said Mace, "Five Bennys, one twenty."

Across the table, Owen thrust his hand out his sleeve and exposed the gold Rolex.

"'J.C.C. Jr.' on the back," Owen said.

It was Jack's all right.

"Where's the third guy?" he asked.

"He's the one who hired us."

"He did the kickin'," Mace said. "You got them boot bruises, man?"

Jack allowed that he had.

"How much he pay you guys?" Jack asked.

"He hands us two thou at first."

"That's all?"

"Three more when we finish with you."

"He gave you five, then. You ID the sonovabitch and I'll pay you ten. Okay?"

They looked at each other and nodded.

"Okay. Who was he?"

"Big lean guy. Hispanic. 'Bout sixty, maybe more. Moustache, little beard. Wears a leather cap," Owen said.

"He talks funny, you know." Mace imitated a lisp.

Owen pointed to his throat. "He talks, the Adam's apple jumps up and down. He said to punish you. We punish you. You been a bad boy, Black Jack?"

Alvin was grinning from ear to ear. "Spic pays niggers to whack a white man. Hey, equal opportunity job."

Jack looked at him, his hopes up. "You know him?"

Alvin nodded.

"*Who?*"

"Cost you ten on top of the five, big man. Okay?"

"Okay."

"C'mon. I'll take you to him."

Alvin's eyes were beacons of joy. In the car, he sang the Alvin Anthem:

Money makes the wheels go 'round
Wheels go 'round
Wheels go 'round
Money makes the wheels go 'round
I shit you not.

"I always thought it was love," Jack said.

Alvin had to laugh. "You gotta be kiddin'.'"

The Starlight Club was a roadhouse outside of East St. Louis, its large neon sign lighting up the parking area. Alvin led Jack inside, and went directly through the cocktail lounge to the inner office. At his desk, a dark, slender, gray-haired man was on the phone, his Adam's apple bobbing as Owen had said. Whatever this man's shock at seeing his victim, he showed no signs of it, finishing his call without missing a beat.

"Amigo! Como está?"

"Hey, Señor. Estupendo," Alvin replied.

"And look who's here! Black Jack Cagle!" He spoke the name like one who could not be more delighted.

"Big man, say hello to Carlos Sanguellan."

Jack stiffened, resisting the chill that coursed through him. Sanguellan! Sam's mentor from the tow-truck scam at the flooded base of Webster Hill. He gasped like one who just shook hands with a dead man come back to life.

"My grandson, hey, he worships you. An autograph! Please."

He had a pen at the ready, a note pad on his desk. "To José, okay? When he saw they beat you up, he cried!"

Jack refused the pen. Stunned, he glared at Alvin who was grinning as if this were all a game.

"Hey Señor, we come to do business, okay? We just come from Manny's. Had a beer with Owen and Mace."

"Owen and Mace?" Carlos looked as if he were digging to place them in his head.

"The guys who whacked him," Alvin said. "And they said it was you paid them to do it."

Carlos was nothing but curious.

"Now why would they say that?"

"Hey Carlos, this is Black Jack Cagle. He pays big bucks to find out what he has to find out."

"I see. He wants to know. If somebody did that to me, I'd do the same."

"Now he wants to know one more name, Carlos."

"Of course. Like I said, I'd do the same."

"He'll pay big bucks, Carlos."

Sanguellan nodded, looked at Jack for confirmation.

Jack was ready for him.

"Ten thousand dollars," he said.

Carlos was at the top of his game. He shook his head. After all, Jack had offended him, hadn't he.

"You'll have to double it, kid. I'm thinking maybe you think you already know. Hey, it's Carlos Sanguellan, it rings a bell, eh? But if you don't pay for what I'm gonna tell you, you'll never really know, will you."

"Okay. Twenty thousand."

"*And* the autograph to my grandson."

Suddenly it was Jack's turn to smile. He stared at Sanguellan while he wrestled with his decision. A moment like this, it can turn out as sweet as honey if it comes from the gut.

"Sorry," he said, his voice totally without rancor.

Sanguellan raised his hands, resigned to defeat.

"Sam Manning." Sanguellan spoke the name as it had no greater consequence that an answer to a trivia question. He smiled, too, as if he would have told him for nothing.

Jack was stunned, not by the spoken name but the boldness of Sanguellan's betrayal. It made no sense. He began to suspect Sanguellan was lying. Why would he snitch on Sam?

"Hard to believe, eh?" Sanguellan teased him. "Hey, it was a favor to my old amigo. He needed the job fast. Bing bang boom. One day you're making waves, that night you're out of it."

"Suppose he finds out you fingered him?"

"Hey, I'm gonna tell him myself! He'll say, yeah yeah, it's like having it both ways. Twenty big ones? He'll laugh. This bothers you, kid? What do you think you're gonna do, have me arrested? Get Sam arrested? He denies, I deny. And you're the sucker, kid. Nobody can fuck with Sam. I give you the ABC, kid: A: Sam was born smart. B: He learned how to use the smarts from Carlos Sanguellan. And, you wanna

know C? You keep messing with him, we do a recap on your fuckin'
face!" He laughed big this time. "On *your* money!"

Alvin drove Jack back to the St. Louis airport for his car rental.
"They gonna trust you with all that money, Alvin?"
"They got no choice, man."
"Suppose you don't give it to them. Suppose you tell them it was
me who didn't pay."
Alvin shook his head like one who couldn't believe what he'd
just heard.
"Dead beat is dead meat, big man." Alvin looked hard at Jack. "You
just gotta trust me."
Jack nodded. He trusted him all right. Besides, he, too, had no
choice.
"Gandee Square, tomorrow. Three o'clock."
"I'll tell you a secret, man."
"What?"
"I'll be there in the square."
Jack nodded. "No show, no dough."

His hotel suite had the musty smell of an old damp sofa. It went
with the sight of the tacky carpeting, the torn, stained wallpaper. This
was the Hotel Gandee, and though he had know it all his life, it was
the first time he had ever been inside. He had chosen not to go home,
not while he was on a mission he couldn't explain even to himself.
He stood at the window overlooking the square, taking in familiar
sights from a lofty angle. The top of Colonel Gandee's hat was splattered with decades of accumulated pigeon shit. Empty beer cans and torn
magazines were scattered around rooftops, under them, several stores no
longer in business. Stark's Department Store, for instance. He remembered Billy Ray Stark, always the best-dressed kid in high school. Where
and when did they go? Deland's Jewelry Store was now a video shop. He
remembered Mr. Deland with the magnifying glass cupped in his eye
peering into an open wristwatch. Everything seemed worn out, needing a fresh coat of paint, or a newly-planted shrub in the slotted whiskey barrels by the curb. When he had come home for Black Jack Field,
the bunting and flags and welcome signs had concealed the worst of it.
Now Main Street reflected the despair that had brought him back.
Finally, the phone rang. It would be Gordon returning his call,
Jack knew, in flight to L.A.

"You're still in Gandee?" Gordon sounded as if such a thing could not possibly be.

Jack had no desire to discuss this. "Gordon, can you transfer five million dollars to the Bank of Gandee?"

"Can I do what?"

"All right, I'll repeat it: I want you—"

"Why? What are you talking about?"

"Gordon!"

"Where is Judith? Let me talk to Judith."

"Then call her in L.A. tonight. Meanwhile, I want that five million doll—"

"You're joking, kid. We'll talk about it tomorrow. I'll call you as soon as I get in."

He was determined not to get steamed up. He wanted to do business the way business was supposed to be done. It was his money. His money. "When you get to L.A., Gordon, make whatever arrangements you think best, but I want five million—"

"You didn't hear me the other day, did you? I tried to explain something to you about money. I thought I made myself clear. As I recall, you agreed, or did I get it wrong?"

"Look, I don't want to—"

"If I'm going to take care of your interests, kid, all such matters must be thoroughly thrashed out. I don't tell you how to pitch. You don't tell me what to do with your money."

He knew this was going to happened, which, as it turned out, simply shortened his fuse.

He was not only ready, but eager.

"Gordon, you get that money here by noon tomorrow, or you're fuckin' fired!"

Silence. Beautiful, soul-satisfying silence. Then, at last, the first tentative response:

"I'm going to pretend you never said that, kid."

"Okay, I'll say it again. Ready?"

"That won't be necessary. Suppose you tell me what you're planning to do?"

"That's my business, not yours. Your business is to do what I ask. So do it!"

And to punctuate the command, he slammed the receiver so Gordon could hear that too.

What else could he possible tell him? That a goggle-eyed black-ass runt had introduced him to a whole new concept of the meaning of happiness? All his life Jack had been told what to do and he did it. It could be said that he'd never had an original thought, that his hundred-mile-an-hour fastball was better than any idea he could possibly have. Now, everything had gone crazy. He was at a frightening fork in the road, alone in a dingy hotel room in a crisis so weird it all but bursted his hump. But in all his twenty-seven years he had never felt more alive.

For the first time in his life he was excited by an idea.

("When you've got the dough, they don't say no.")

He was going to have Sam Manning's head, whatever it cost.

Inside the Bank of Gandee, the sun ran a streak of light from a lofty window forming a golden spot on the polished tile floor. Muted music floated through the air like an organ in a cathedral. Jack remembered how, when he was a boy, all sounds were hushed in the bank. Even as they approached the building, his father would begin to speak in subdued tones. Banks intimidated him, even now when he could have owned one. On the other hand, he had never walked into a locker room he didn't like.

Henry Ullman, the bank manager, was a trim dapper man in his mid-fifties—perfectly barbered, neat pencil-thin moustache, every gray hair on his head properly set. If ever a man could command respect for the diligence of his grooming, Henry Ullman was such a man. Those who knew him best admitted that he cared little about anything else— except, of course, the affairs of the bank. Compared to Jack, in casual jeans, sport shoes, blue-gray Gortex jacket, Ullman seemed like a model for a Beverly Hills mortuary. But if Jack had been worried whether his five million dollars was safely there, all such concerns were dispelled by Ullman's greeting. Even the moustache was twitching with excitement.

"What a pleasure to see you, my boy! We've all been concerned about your misfortune. I must say, though: those bruises do add to your image."

"A pleasure to see *you*, Mr. Ullman."

"When you pitched in the Babe Ruth League, you fanned my son twice in one game. Neither he nor I will ever forget that. Even then, your fast ball would dance a bit. Even then!"

"Can we get down to business?" Jack asked.

"Certainly. And five million dollars is a lot of business!"

Immediately, he began to move papers on his desk. "What sort of account do you wish?" He smiled again. "My staff has a pool going already. Do you intend to build a hospital? A community center? A scholarship fund, perhaps? Forgive the speculation, my boy."

"No, sir. Nothing like that." Jack paused, shrugged. "I thought I'd have a little fun with it."

Ullman looked so befuddled, Jack laughed. Then he requested fifty thousand dollars in five-thousand-dollar stacks of hundred dollar bills. And did the bank have a case for him to carry it in?

Ullman assured him, no problem.

"Money makes the wheels go 'round," Jack said when everything was properly arranged.

"Doesn't it though."

Across the square, Alvin was sitting on the hood of his Chevy, feet resting on the bumper. Jack smiled in greeting.

"Alvin, what in hell are *you* doing here?"

"Ain't this Gandee, the most beautiful town in the great state of Missouri? Lots of kindly hard-working folk with them family values?"

"You bet."

Alvin gestured to the brief case.

"Got your lunch in there, big man?"

"Pair of old shoes, a towel I stole from the hotel, some dirty laundry."

Alvin was opening the car door. "Let's go into my office. I might be interested in that towel."

Jack set the brief case on his lap, opened it for Alvin to see.

"Ta da," Jack said.

Alvin took a stack, riffled it by his ear. "Feels like an angel's kiss."

"You did real good, Alvin."

"Big man, when you need another push, call me."

"Gonna make the wheels go 'round."

"When you've got the dough, you make the flow."

The little man was playing with the stacks like a kid with a stash of chocolate bars. "I go to Sanguellan with twenty, then Manny's with ten." He was laughing now. "Then I take the rest of the day off."

Jack stepped out of the Chevy and said goodbye. "I love you, Alvin."

"Couldn't want for no more than that."

At the Gandee Diner, he was amused by his face in the huge mirror. This was mugging day plus four, and he was still an atrocity with dark bruises around puffed up eyes, his upper lip so fat as to distort the curl of his moustache. There was a copy of the *Sentinel* on the counter with his hospital picture on the front page. He looked pathetic. He no longer raged at the beating but treated it as a badge of honor. That   this was Gandee, not the World Series, made it seem all the better. Even sitting at this counter drinking coffee out of a stained white mug was perfect.

Lila saw him looking and had to tease him. "You're so pretty, Jack."

He shrugged. "Some got it, some don't."

"The shiners are classy," Lila went on.

"Makes me look like a raccoon."

"You look to me like someone who wants to kick some ass."

"It crossed my mind," he admitted.

"This town is more into ass-*kissing*, if you know what I mean."

"No different than most places."

"My guess is that if there was a contest, Gandee would win the gold."

"Lila, what are you doing in this town anyway?"

"Well, it was like this. I was on this raft heading down the Mississippi to Mardi Gras. Storm came up, we capsized in white water, rescued from sea monsters by a millionaire in a yacht. He took me to Gandee, bought me the diner, and it was happy ever after. How's that?"

"More coffee, please."

She laughed, refilled his mug.

"What are *you* doing here, Jack?"

He almost told her.

She shoved the *Sentinel* in front of him.

"Here, read all about how you got mugged. Biggest news in Gandee since Sam Manning opened a car door for an old lady."

"Do you know Hector Quaid, Lila?"

"Owns the *Sentinel?*"

"Yeah. What's he like?"

"Ask Foxx."

"I'm asking you."

"He's like a B.L.T. with one slice of bacon."

Jack laughed, "On what kind of bread?"

She considered that for a moment. "Burnt toast."

Jack looked at the mirror again, this time to see the *Sentinel* window across the square with the letters *L E N I T N E S*. He remembered seeing them backwards when he was inside the offices, in grade school

on a field trip to learn about "making the news." All those side-by-side
cubicles, editors at computers, telephones going, and then he had
watched hundreds of copies come rolling off the press.

Now Foxx would be there. And for Jack, that would make all the
difference.

He found Hector Quaid at his home on Baxter Street. The old
house was set well back from the road, leaves were raked on a weedless
lawn, hedges were neatly trimmed. Jack used the polished brass rapper
on the door rather than the doorbell.

In seconds, there stood Hector's wiry body and bony face. When
he saw who it was, he was bowled over.

"It's young Cagle, Celia!" He called over his shoulder.

Lean and gray, she looked like she might be Hector's sister than
his wife.

They'd been playing dominoes, Jack saw.

"Sorry to interrupt your game," he said.

"Not at all. Celia, why don't you make a pot of tea."

Jack held up his hand to stop her. "Not a social call, Mr. Quaid. I'd
rather get right at this."

Quaid looked up, somewhat startled.

"I'm here to buy the *Sentinel*," Jack said.

"What! What on earth for?"

"Let's talk money, Mr. Quaid."

"Look here, son. I'm not at all sure the paper is for sale."

Jack smiled. "The way I understand this sort of thing, *everything* is
for sale. Just a matter of how much."

"Yes, I've heard the story about that woman of questionable virtue.
Nonetheless—"

"How's $250,000, Mr. Quaid?"

Immediately, Jack saw that he had him. Quaid's necktie jumped as
he swallowed. The burnt toast had crumbled at the first touch of the
butter knife.

"Well, I'll certainly consider the offer, son. You see, Celia here is
part owner—"

"Sure. Talk it over. We can write up a letter of agreement. I'll give
you a check. Take fifteen minutes, Mr. Quaid. No reason to beat this
around, is there?"

As it happened, the Quaid's came back to the living room in ten, a
quickly typed letter in hand. Together with Jack's personal check, it
would serve its temporary purposes.

The old publisher, however, was bubbling with curiosity. What was this all about?

"Don't much like the comics," Jack said.

"Why, that's all syndicated, son. There's not much choice."

"Tell you the truth, sir, I always had a hankering to do those drawings myself."

Quaid stared at him, suddenly realizing that Jack was putting him on. Obviously something far more important was happening here.

"A bit of advice, son: don't bite off more than you can chew."

"My father says, 'the bigger the bite, the more you get to eat.'"

Quaid shook his head, offering his best it's-your-funeral smile. Jack turned to leave before the proverbial ink was dry.

He had bought the *Sentinel* in less time than it took him to buy a pair of shoes.

J ack sat behind Hector Quaid's polished oak desk, swiveled in the leather high-backed chair to stare at the diner across the square through the huge *L E* window. Now he owned the *Sentinel*, but it was like buying an airplane without knowing how to fly. He was counting on Foxx to be his pilot.

Then there she was in the doorway pretending to be Little Red Riding Hood.

"My, what big black eyes you have, Mr. Quaid. And when did you grow the swirling black moustache?"

"Sit down, Foxx. Sit down."

She didn't move. "I'm due at the dog pound in twenty minutes. We're doing a special on the new dog catcher."

"Please." He gestured to the chair.

She wanted some answers first.

"What's this all about, Jack?"

"For one thing, you were right about the mugging, Foxx."

"So?"

He tried to explain why he had gotten off the plane, struggling to find the right words for complicated emotions. He told her about Alvin, then led her through the mess with Owen and Mace, and finally the incredible confrontation with Sanguellan.

"It was Sam!" he said. "Jesus, he's no better than a goddam thug!"

Foxx never budged from the door jamb, never batted an eye. It was as if she knew it all along.

"I still don't understand, Jack."

"I bought the paper. We're gonna knock the sonovabitch out of the box. We're gonna elect a new mayor!"

"May I ask who?"

"D.D."

"In less than two weeks?"

"Why not?"

"Be real, Jack. Last I heard, Sam has most of the 2,665 registered voters by the well-known."

Jack smiled. "Sit down, Foxx. Please."

This time she sat, a concession to his quiet intensity.

"Suppose the *Sentinel* takes him on, Foxx. We expose him every way imaginable. The corrupt kickback deals, that toxic land deal, the bribes, whatever else you guys can dig up. We run a special edition with the whole story of Sam's corruption, the way he steals from the town. We open up the whole can of worms."

She shrugged. "He'll still be re-elected."

Jack was like a poker player about to turn up a royal flush.

"Page one, Foxx: It reads 'On the day D.D. is elected mayor by write-in, the town of Gandee will receive a million dollars for the redevelopment of small business on Main Street, another million dollars for the restoration of Clark Street, still another million for a college scholarship fund.'" Then, as she absorbed these numbers, he added his clincher: "And to sweeten the offer: 'For every registered voter, a check for five hundred dollars.'"

She began to work it over behind tightly-pressed lips and furrowed brow, her head moving this way and that. Her seated body exuded tension like one about to leap out of her chair. He waited, sweating her out. What could he do without her? Without her, he was a cannon without ammo.

Finally, she got to her feet and moved toward the door.

"Foxx!" he barked. "Goddammit, where do you think you're going!"

She stopped in the doorway. "Hardball is a team sport, Jack." She held up her hand, a sit-tight gesture. She'd be back with the staff.

Including Foxx, there were five. Mary Ellen Lacey was a middle-aged woman who spoke in whispery tones like one frightened of her own words. As it turned out, however, she was as tough as nails. Lloyd Seneca was bright-eyed, eager, his pen and note pad at the ready. Warren Chasins was a heavy-set round-faced man around forty, his steel-rimmed glasses perched on his bald pate ready to flip over his eyes like an outfielder in the sun-field. Ben Tucker was a bearded black man, prematurely graying, the only one of the four who did not smile at Foxx's introduction. They immediately took seats in the spacious office, and then there was quiet as they sat, a mixed bag of stares that suggested uneasy pickings.

Only Foxx was smiling. "Play ball, Jack!" she said.

He took a deep breath and began his pitch. The *Sentinel* would be his tool to deliver the message, as he had told Foxx. In one special edition, they would make magic happen. When he finished, a long ominous silence was broken by Warren Chasins.

"What it gets down to, you want to buy the election."

So, the first reaction was negative, and it hit Jack like a bad call from an umpire.

"You have a problem with that?" Jack challenged him.

"I most certainly do. It puts a very bad taste in my mouth," Chasins replied.

And immediately Ben Tucker jumped on board. "People won't believe this kind of giveaway. On Clark Street, black people don't like Sam, but they sure as hell don't trust Jack. Are you really gonna spend all that money? This is Gandee, Cagle. They'll think it's bullshit."

"So it's the money that turns you off, Mr. Tucker?"

"Like Warren says, I get a bad taste."

"This is bad news," Warren went on. "You'll be swimming with sharks, you know what I mean? This is Sam Manning we'd be going after!"

Then from across the room, Mary Ellen challenged him.

"So what's he going to do, Warren? Burn down the building?"

"Just look at Cagle's face. I for one don't care to look like that!" Saying that, Warren sent his own snowball rolling downhill. "Look, this is out of our league. It's crazy. Jack may own the paper but Sam owns Gandee. The people won't go with this. Even if we go to press, the paper will never hit the streets. Sam will never let it happen."

"I say we forget it!" said Ben Tucker.

Again, silence, this time born out of confusion and doubt. Jack saw them staring at him. The ball was in his court, all right. Without batting an eye, he knew what he had to do.

"Well, the way I see it, I need you. It'll take the whole team to do this. Big jobs deserve big pay, right? So I'm going to double all your salaries. Then I'm going to pay a fifteen-thousand-dollar bonus to each of you on the day this paper goes to press!"

Jack smiled as he watched Warren Chasins rub the back of his neck. Ben Tucker was chewing on his pencil.

"What'll it be, eh?" he asked.

The message was clear enough. If he could buy them, he could buy the voters too. End of debate. Right?

("When you've got the dough, they don't say no.")

"You've made your point, Cagle," Chasins said.

Jack smiled.

"Call me Jack. Okay?"

He had to clear the air of all doubts. He had to do this thing, he told them. He had bought the paper to make it possible. Everything in Gandee was going to be different.

"You people, you're all pros, but you've been writing stuff about busted traffic lights and the Fourth of July parade from the firehouse. Okay. But now you're going to kick ass. This is going to be a real newspaper. I tell you, I came back to Gandee, I didn't know shit about anything. I gave two million bucks for the ball field, and I'm ashamed of what happened with it. What you've got to know is I don't give a good goddam what Sam is going to do to stop us. I'm not going to quit. I'm not leaving until Ruby Coles is free and Sam is through!"

And when he saw that they were all with him, he turned the meeting over to Foxx.

It was as if she were born for this moment. Her eyes sparkled with fresh fire as she went into action. Her body became catlike with energy rising to infect them all. First she had Jack recounting his confrontations. Then she gave assignments to each of them. Mary Ellen would visit Ruby in prison. Ben Tucker would work with Lorene over the drug connections. Warren Chasins would chase down the kickbacks in the building of Black Jack Field. Lloyd Seneca would investigate the toxic field problems. They were all to conduct tough interviews and get incriminating quotes. No holds barred! They would put together an issue of the *Sentinel* that would read like a declaration of war. Everything was dominated by Jack's ultimate goal: "*Sam must go!*"

And so it went for four days and four nights—the team became an unstoppable force. Years of pathetic indifference, writing pat-a-cake stories, now turned into a stirring busyness they had never believed possible. Office lights flooded the square through all hours, another message that this was no ordinary week. The response was gratifying. When the first bits of information began to leak into rumors, one word led to another. Whatever the old fears of reprisal, once the momentum began, the *Sentinel* force became a rolling snowball.

Through these turbulent days, Jack watched the action flow around him. At first bewildered like one who couldn't speak the language, he quickly learned to participate. He knew what he wanted and made certain no one ever forgot it. He even wrote his own "Declaration of Intent" as a lead editorial, a blunt, no-nonsense, hard-assed statement that made everything else more believable. "All my life I thought my uncle was a wonderful guy. Then, all at once, I found out that he was a crook and a liar. It was like your best friend had raped your wife." It was the first time he had written anything since high school.

Then came the day they would go to press. The staff met in Jack's office as Foxx laid out the issue for them. Under a commanding "Sam Must Go!" headline, there was his grinning face surrounded by the statement of his seven deadly sins: *Drug Dealing! Bribery! Extortion! Fraud! Racism! Blackmail! Mendacity!* Inside, one by one, each sin was documented by an interview specifying charges. They all responded to each with mounting enthusiasm. It was a time of self-congratulation, like a team that had just won the pennant, lacking only the playful spraying of champagne, until, suddenly, there came a slow, singular, rhythmic clapping that threatened the room like distant thunder in the middle of a picnic.

They turned to see Sam Manning himself, all smiles. Behind him, like a bodyguard, stood Sheriff John Clyde Cagle Sr.

Jack gasped at this preposterous intrusion. Sam, of course, was in seventh heaven. The *Sentinel* staff paled and went silent.

Sam took the floor as if he owned them all, permitting no challenge to his presence. His eyes fastened on Jack. No one else interested him.

"You gotta be jokin' with this garbage," he said, pointing to the papers on the desk. "You don't know what you're doin', kid." Sam's tone was a warning now, his voice promising disaster. "Sam ain't goin' nowhere!"

Then, after a petrifying pause: "But *you* are, kid. *You* are!"

Jack would have loved to take him on but he had no idea how. What could he say? What cards was Sam holding? It would be like calling a man's bluff then watching him turn up a full house.

Sam wasted no time with it. "You got interviews? You got tapes?" He was asking questions like a movie gangster with a gun in a man's face. "Well so do I, kid."

The silence was breathless now. It was as if they'd been taken over by Satan himself. They stared at Sam as he set his own tape recorder on the desk, then pushed the "on" button.

They heard the sound of a nervous young girl reading a prepared statement, the texture of which seemed so preposterous that it gradually became credible.

"My name is Vicki Comminger. I am fifteen years old and live at 61 Clark Street, Gandee, Missouri. Last summer, I was visiting my aunt in Chicago when the Dodgers were playing there. Since I came from the same hometown as Black Jack Cagle, I thought it would be fun to get his autograph. I went to his hotel, the Hilton, and called him from the lobby. He said sure. Room 1414. At first he was nice. He said he would give me his autograph, no problem, but I would have to do something for him first. I said, sure, what was it? He said, 'Give me head, honey.' Then he took off his pants. Then he grabbed me. He tried to force me to do things. And when I tried to back away, he hit me in the face. I kept saying no, no. He ripped off my clothes and beat me up bad. Then he raped me!"

"Had enough?" said the mayor, pushing the "off" button.

"I've done some checking around, kid. I must say, you have quite a rep. You seem to have attracted young girls in swarms! I'm sure there'll be a substantial response to this tape, if you know what I mean. Like they say, you've got some mighty big stats in the sex department!"

Silence again. Never was a room so crowded with living flesh and so completely silent. Finally, it was broken by a plaintive sigh from Mary Ellen. "Oh, God."

The mayor wore a sad sympathetic face as if this were all too painful even for him.

"Colored gal," he went on. "Didn't know you liked the dark meat that much, kid."

Not only rape, but race. The old one-two. And a minor for three.

Jack felt completely impotent about denying it, though no black girl had ever come to his suite in Chicago or anywhere else. He had never attacked any woman, ever, nor even fantasized about doing so. For all his countless affairs, his sexual history was completely devoid of assault. He'd never had reason. But any such denial would have played right into the mayor's slimy hands.

It took his gleaming spit-and-polished father to use this moment to bury him.

"Son, I'm ashamed of you!" The voice of the hero sounded as if he could hardly cope with that shame.

"I must say, kid, I am too." Sam was like an army tank crashing through the jungle. "I didn't want to believe this. What could be more destructive than this! I thought, how could you be so careless! Believe me, I had little Vicki's story investigated. Aunt in Chicago. A long talk with the poor little girl herself. She's frightened, and she's angry. Can't blame her, you know."

Sam was playing with him in front of his staff, a few sly rounds of cat-and-mouse before he actually bit Jack's head off.

"Look, kid, I'm real sorry this had to happen. Then there's that rowdy history of yours. That wild night in Texas? At the Alamo, was it? You did some time, didn't you? With that colored roommate of yours? Am I right? You've got to admit, you overstepped your Black Jack image. You can see what we're dealing with, kid. I mean, this could be dynamite!"

"What else, Sam? There's more, ain't there?"

"Come to think of it, yeah. I thought it best to advise your boss of this, you know. This Pagonis, he's a smart man. When he heard the tape, he went right to the heart of it. 'What do you want, Mr. Mayor?' he said. That's all: 'What do you want?' And you know what I answered, kid? I answered, 'Mr. Pagonis, you *get that rapist sonovabitch out of my town* and I promise you total silence!'"

The mayor took a moment to pick lint off his sleeve like one who couldn't get on with his life until every bit was removed.

"It comes down to a little old quid pro quo. Cut your losses, kid. You get your ass out of town and we wipe the slate clean. You've got to see the sense of that. You made a bad mistake. No big deal. Hey, everybody makes mistakes. You drop this stuff in the *Sentinel*. There'll be none of that! I'll drop this here tape. No *Sentinel*, no Vicki. No one will know. I promised your boss. Not a peep. You following me, kid? I'll venture to say these good people here can see the sense of it. You head back to L.A. where it's all sunshine and happy-happy. When you get off that plane, that lady of yours will be waiting for you with open arms. And, hey, what's so terrible about that?" Then, turning to the sheriff: "You agree, John?"

Jack's father had all he could do to contain his anger.

"Best you leave town, Son!"

"I'll be in my office, kid."

And then they were gone, leaving the staff feeling as if they had witnessed an execution.

Finally, then, the big question. "What's it going to be, boss?" All eyes settled on the man behind the desk.

He couldn't answer. His defense was a question of his own. "Who's gonna believe that bullshit?" But, even as he asked, routine images of disaster came flying by. Star-hero rape always plays well because it was so much fun to play with. God knows, hundred-million-dollar ballplayers are fair game. One call from the mayor's office to any TV station in St. Louis would release the sordid details to the networks. Sweet little Vicki would suddenly appear out of nowhere and deliver the message live. Into the pot would jump the tabloids and gossip junksters. Compromising old pictures of Black Jack partying would be dug out of newspaper morgues. Suddenly, fifty other girls of all racial extractions would surface with Black Jack sex stories, some with whom he had actually bedded and some who merely wished, but who cared? It would all be super nasty. And then, you could bet on it, there would be a pretty blond fourteen-year-old boy.

The phone rang, cracking the silence like a thunderclap. Foxx reached for it. "The *Sentinel*," she said.

"Give me Cagle!" The voice was a command, clearly audible throughout the room. It was Pagonis, Jack knew. Not a secretary but the man himself. In his car, maybe. Or his bathroom.

Jack took the phone and prepared himself for the onslaught.

"What is this nonsense?" Pagonis cried out.

"That tape is a damn lie. It never happened!"

"I don't give a shit, Jack. And neither does the mayor. That tape is a gun at your head. What do you think you're doin' anyway? You bought a newspaper? What the hell is that? You're the greatest ballplayer in the goddam world and you're playin' politics in that stinkin' little town? That man scares me, Jack. He's a smart sonovabitch who knows all the moves. I'm gonna say this once: You do exactly what he tells you to do. You fold that goddam newspaper and get out of there. You hear me, Jack? Jack, do you hear me?"

"Yes, sir."

He hung up knowing that everyone must have heard. There would be no mystery to the call. They sat there waiting for the word.

"What are we supposed to do?" Chasins asked.

Jack shook his head. "I don't know."

"We're not going to quit, are we?" Mary Ellen was incredulous.

"This is bullshit!" Ben Tucker snapped.

Jack turned to the window, helpless to defend himself. He heard them leave but he refused to watch them go. When he looked back, only Foxx was there. She seemed too tired to get up. When she looked up at him, her lips were shut tight as if to prevent any words from coming out. He could see the contempt in her eyes. At any minute, he guessed, words would come blasting away at him.

"Don't bother, Foxx. I know what you're thinking."

"I promise you: it's *worse*."

"What in hell am I supposed to do!" he snapped at her.

"That's *your* problem, Jack."

"I don't have a choice, do I!"

"Hah! So you *do* know. So you're quitting."

"I know this much: money makes the wheels go 'round."

"That's the real trouble, isn't it? You go wherever those wheels take you because that's where the money is. That's all that matters, isn't it?"

She got up, finally, and stood there looking at him.

"Hey, you're the great Black Jack Cagle, the hundred-million-dollar Mean Man. Sure, Sam was smart enough to use it. Raping that little black girl would be right up your alley because that's the image they're selling. But try to be a good guy and they lynch you with your own rope."

She'd had enough of this.

"I'd sure hate to be you, Jack."

And then she was gone.

As he opened his hotel room door the phone was ringing, and then he heard Corky's voice on the answering machine.

"So, it seems you stepped in shit, hey?"

Jack picked up the phone.

"I didn't see where I was going, Corky."

"Change your shoes and start all over."

"That what Junior says?"

"He wants to know if he's got an uncle like that."

"Judith thinks he's cute. Like a doll, she says."

"Wind it up and it kills you."

"Tell Junior that if he's a bad boy my uncle will come to baby sit."

"What's it gonna be, Roomie?"

"I got a bottle. Thought I might drink about it."

"Hey, that's funny."

"Million laughs."

"Best you mosey on home, man."

"Yeah, we could have a catch in your driveway."

"Shoot some pool."

"Shit sure happens, Corky."

"Hey, it's the off-season, remember?"

Jack left the phone for the window, one final look over what had to be the most pathetic week of his life. He now knew one thing: this was not his kind of game. Let them have the fucking town. It's theirs not his. He was a fool to come back. He was doomed when he did but he didn't know it, which marked him as all the more stupid. He'd gone so far out of his league that Sam would have everyone laughing at him.

Jack must go! he said to himself. Go! Get you ass where it belongs. Call Judith and be thankful that you finally came to your senses.

He could handle the bad shit now, apologize to Foxx, pay off the staff, wish D.D. the best, but there'd be no promises to the people about money. Jack was through.

Only one thing seemed necessary: he had to square it with his father. He saw that clearly. Then, like one suddenly inspired, he began to think that maybe he could turn his father to his side. Maybe he would convince his father there was no cause for shame, there was only Sam's insidious violation of the truth. Jack would not only purge himself, he would make his father an ally. And maybe, just maybe, together they might turn this whole mess into a victory.

Jack sat beside the sheriff's desk, watching his father read a letter. Finally the sheriff dropped the letter into his file basket and turned to his son.

"So what's up, Son?"

Jack went right to the heart of it.

"I never raped that girl, Dad."

The sheriff was unimpressed. "Vicki Comminger was prepared to swear that you did. I was there at the taping, Son."

"Look, Dad, it was a set up. Sam had to do something to stop me."

"That may be so, but I believed her."

"I don't rape women, Dad. I never even saw that girl!"

"Everybody's lyin' but you, that right?"

"Sam's a liar, and a lot worse!"

"You think that, and that makes everything easy, don't it? You know something? That's the way you live. You think what you want, you do what you want. You expect to get away with whatever."

"I didn't do it, Dad."

"Okay. You didn't do it."

"That don't sound like you believe me."

"What's the damned difference if I do or I don't. Like I said, that's the way you live."

"Jesus, you're my father. You shouldn't be tellin' me you're ashamed of it."

The sheriff looked at his watch, obviously wanting no more of this. Jack was so far from getting what he wanted, his stomach rumbled in protest.

"There's more, Dad. Goddammit, it was Sam who had me mugged!"

The sheriff stared at him, shook his head, laughed.

"When you get started, you don't stop, do you."

"Carlos Sanguellan, Dad. He told me!"

"You paid him, didn't you? A sucker paid a crook. You ain't nothin' but a damned fool, Son. God's gift to America, ain't you. To me, you're the same damned fool you always was. You come back here, you think you're better than the rest of us. But you ain't. Best you remember that I made you. You sure as hell ain't better than me, and you never will be." All this came spilling out, oozing contempt like a man who had never lost at anything.

"Sam's a fuckin' thief, goddammit!"

"Don't you dare use that kinda talk in this office! That's what's happened to you. Just look at you. Hair down to your neck, that stupid moustache. 'Black Jack.' What kinda name is that? Like you're a damn nigger! I can't believe you're my son. I don't give a hoot in hell how much money you have. You're a class A idiot! You had your big night at the field, you should've quit right there. You came back for what? You care so much for the nigger wife? You gotta be even dumber than you ever was! You may be a hero to the rest of the world but like I said, I'm ashamed of you!"

His father's voice became a gathering of strange sounds, sometimes whining, sometimes oozing fear. There was no compassion, no love, no capacity to understand, only the arrogance of a man demanding that everything give way before him.

The sheriff then reached for another letter, set it meticulously on the desk top as he returned his glasses to his face as if this were an earth-shaking document he had to deal with.

Jack watched him, burning him with his eyes. Let him read the fucking letter, or pretend to. And the next one. Whatever. Jack knew that this was going to be his moment to make something happen.

"I got things to do, Son."

Jack was ready for him.

"You're full of shit, Dad. It's all over your lyin' face. You're so scared you even lie like a coward. You're no sheriff, you're a goddam empty uniform. All you do is cover up for Sam and his fuckin' lies. I can hear you sucking, Dad. 'Hey, Sam, you swindlin' big bucks in the Black Jack Field deals? Hey, no problem. You got Starger movin' in drugs for a piece of your action? Hey, lotsa luck! You bangin' a real estate lady in Overton who fronts for you? Hey, I see nothin'!' That ain't a sheriff, Dad, that's a goddam lackey! That makes you an asshole, Dad. Sam has turned the great war hero into a fuckin' asshole!"

The sheriff didn't budge or bat an eye. It was as if Jack's tirade amused him.

"You all through, Son?" Then, pointing: "There's the door."

Jack saw his insidious smile. His father could laugh at him because there was nothing Jack could do. The confrontation would end where it began. All the words had come to nothing. He made it to the door then suddenly stopped, blocked by the realization that if he left now he'd be everything his father had said he was. He looked back at that smile, baffled by it, seeing something that went beyond gloating over his mastery. Jack had never seen the likes of it. There was a secret in that smile. His father was confessing a secret even as he concealed it. And suddenly Jack saw it for what it was, an insight that horrified him, and the words rose screaming in his throat, exploding in the air like no other sounds he'd ever made:

"You killed him! Holy God, you killed Cyrus!"

His father stopped reading the letter and looked at him.

The secret was gone but the pleasure remained.

"Just take it easy, Son."

"Christ, *it was you!*"

There was no denial. His father saw no need for it.

"You were leaving, Son? Goodbye."

"You hated him? He was coming to see me and you had to stop him!"

"Yes, I had to stop him. For your own good, Son. Who needed that fat nigger at your ball park? Who knew what he'd say on the TV. You should thank me! I made the evening work. Until you threw that sissy pitch to me, it was perfect!"

The sheriff never lost a second of his smile. Whatever it signified, whatever he had done, it meant nothing to him. He took pleasure from still another chance to demonstrate his power.

"Oh my God!" Jack cried out.

"He was a no-good fat-assed nigger about to tell my wimpy son a lot of crap about this town he didn't have to hear. I tried to stop him, nice and friendly-like. 'Turn around and go home, Cyrus!' I tell him. He don't listen. The nigger laughs in my face. He says somethin' about how you owe him money and he's gonna get it back no matter what! I don't get with no nigger laughin' at me, not for anything. He starts his van up like I ain't even there. No sheriff I ever heard of stand for that!"

Jack shut his eyes, remembering the five dollars.

"He was gonna ruin your night, maybe make a nigger race hate protest on the TV. You didn't need that. The town didn't need that. By God, I'd do it again! Killing is surgery, you cut out the cancer."

Jack was staggered by this onslaught. His father was out of his mind. Surgery? Cancer? This was *murder!*

"You'll get convicted. You'll go to the chair!"

Again the arrogance: "Nobody saw nothin', Son. No witness. No evidence. No reason to worry: nobody can put the finger on me."

"Just another dead nigger," Jack said.

"No reason to make anything of it," the sheriff agreed. "Like you doin' your dumb newspaper thing, no one is gonna care 'bout that neither, one way or another. And now that you're leavin', I can tell you, everybody'll be a whole lot happier."

Jack was seething, fists clenched, his eyes shooting bullets of rage. His father saw this and calmly reached for an aluminum baseball bat beside his desk.

"Don't do anything stupid, Son."

"You'd use that on me, Dad?"

"Hey, I love all kinds of weapons. Even when I don't need 'em. Weapons are friends."

Jack shuddered at where these words were leading them, the more frightening for his father's smile.

"You ain't gonna do nothin', son. You ain't healed enough to handle even a fist in those ribs, ain't it right? Like they say, you win some and you lose some. Well, you sure as hell lost. With all your money and big shot ideas, you couldn't beat us. What it comes down to, even an 'asshole' can handle a damned fool." He had to chuckle at his thought if only to rub it in. "No use cussin' no more, Son. Go home. Go home."

Jack glared at him, wanting to challenge him with his eyes, a defiant look that said this wasn't going to be the end of it. But his father denied him even that, and so the scene ended.

Jack turned to leave, hurrying to get outside like a swimmer who'd been under water too long.

At the diner, Lila pointed to Foxx in a corner booth. She was reading a magazine, so involved that she didn't look up to greet him. He sat down across from her, wondering if he could actually get sensible words out with all that roiling in his gut. He was so loaded with pain, he tried to diffuse it with levity.

"Hey, Foxx, I always wondered; what's your—"

"Hortense."

"What?"

"My name. You wanted to know my name, right?"

"Yeah. Jesus, how did you know?"

"Seemed high time you asked."

"You look tired, Hortense."

"Well, no wonder. After you left the office I tried to run the marathon. Hit the wall at sixteen miles. Sometimes my bag gets too heavy for me. You don't look so good yourself, Jack."

"Too much chasin' my tail, I guess."

Then there was Lila with the pot of coffee.

"What'll it be, Jack?"

He was so far away, he needed time to recognize her presence. She grinned at him. "Me Lila, you Jack."

"He's been chasing his tail," Foxx explained.

"Did he catch it?"

Foxx shrugged. "He'd only have to let it go. Dog's law of nature."

Suddenly, startlingly, Black Jack erupted. When he spoke, his words had to fight their way through clamped jaws. His rage was so great, for the first time since childhood, he began to stammer.

"The s-s-sonvab-b-bitch *killed him!* He k-k-killed him then, Jesus, he *p-p-put the widow in jail for it!*"

It was as if he had confronted an evil too powerful for words.

Lila backed away. Foxx pushed the magazine aside and waited for him. Jack took her glass of water and drank it, then pressed the cool glass against his forehead.

Then he told her what had happened, the entire scene in the sheriff's office exactly as he had lived it. He repeated his father's words, even sounding like him, until he came the full circle with his emotions and the horror of what it meant. His heart was beating hard for he had taken himself through a living hell.

When she spoke, out came one word:

"Sisyphus," she said.

"What?"

"The old Greek who had to keep pushing a rock up the hill. The Gods punished him."

"What'd he do?"

"He defied them."

"So he could never make it to the top?"

She shook her head. "Doomed."

He thought about that, vaguely remembering the myth.

"No! No! That ain't me, Foxx!"

"Oh? What'd you have in mind?"

"The *Sentinel*. We go back to work."

"I seem to recall the sad, timid voice of Vicki Comminger."

"Vicki? Who's Vicki?"

"Sometimes you forget too quickly, Jack."

"Hey, if I quit today, I'll hate myself tomorrow."

"And what about after tomorrow? In the office, somebody is going to remind you that Sam Manning always has one more move. Who's going to trust you? And why should we?"

All his life he had never been good with words. From childhood stammering and forever after, he'd never had to rely on what he had to say. But suddenly this was different. Foxx had thought of him as a cop-out from the beginning and now he had to convince her otherwise.

He closed his eyes to let his thoughts settle. So much had happened, he didn't know how to begin until one thought shoved its way to the surface of his mind.

"My father murdered a man with no more reason than you might leave a nickel in a goddam puddle. He just didn't give a damn. He didn't think it mattered. He's the sheriff, Foxx. What kind of shit is that! It's a fuckin' horror! You do a thing like that, you're not human. There's nothin' left of you. I saw what it all came down to. *It was Sam!* Sam had swallowed him up, turned my father into another piece of shit. Sam is poison in the air, Foxx. Hey, like I said, *Sam must go!*"

He stopped for a deep breath, wondering what she was thinking, but she gave no indication, one way or another.

"You were right about me all along, Foxx. What I did to Cyrus and Ruby. If I leave here because of Sam's bullshit lies, I'll never be free of it. I'd have let that sonovabitch walk all over me with this bullshit tape. Can you believe that? Hey, I'll use the tape against him! I'll run it in the *Sentinel*. I'll say, look at what he thinks he can do to me!

"What happened in Gandee? You, that's what. Cyrus, yeah, and Ruby, but mostly you. I gotta tell you, Foxx, I started this and I'm sayin' let's finish it. Okay?"

He stopped, finally, and he guessed that he had just spoken more words in one run than he'd ever spoken his life.

"Okay," she said. That was all. But then her face lit up, and though she tried to maintain her cool, she couldn't come close. "Okay, Jack," she said again.

At the *Sentinel*, the staff went to work behind locked doors. No one was allowed out or in. Foxx was pumped up like one who had just returned from vacation. She had everyone working with non-stop enthusiasm, right around the clock.

Twenty-two hours later, the press began to roll. Jack stood watching, fascinated by the oncoming flood of "Sam Must Go!"s. Foxx pulled a copy and handed it to him, and there was the grinning head shot of Sam Manning in the center of the front page surrounded by the seven deadly sins. Turn the paper over, and the headline read "D.D. for Mayor!"—his picture in the center of his seven living virtues.

Five thousand copies hit the streets just before noon. A fleet of kids on bikes with handlebar baskets loaded fanned out across a dozen roads, supplementing the regular truck route, dropping copies in homes from Clark Street up the hills to Baxter and Sycamore. Others left papers in stores, restaurants, barber shops. Two girls walked through Town Hall itself, a paper for every desk in every office. Stand in the square and you could hear the excitement billowing. The town was electrified. Everyone seemed to know something more to add to the *Sentinel*'s litany of abuses. Above all, they talked about the money. They laughed about the money. Jack had introduced the smartest win/win package ever laid before an electorate: an honest administration to evict a corrupt one, and a neat little nest egg to unite them. Good for morale, great for business.

In the four remaining days before the election, Gandeeans talked of little else. Sam Manning went into battle, sound-trucking through the streets to rally his supporters. He made charges of fraud, the *Sentinel* had lied, Black Jack Cagle could not be trusted, D.D. had no political experience. Sam insisted that he was the greatest mayor the town had ever had.

He didn't have a chance. The election was a write-in landslide. D.D. won over 75 percent of the votes in the largest turnout in Gandee's history, and the town rejoiced as if it were Christmas, New Year's and the Fourth of July rolled into one.

At the *Sentinel*, the offices were like a World Series championship locker room. More champagne was sprayed than drunk. Sounds of laughter and cheers had the windows rattling. Led by the sedate Mary Ellen Lacey, they marched around desks, into one office after another like kids at a birthday party. Ben Tucker simulated a trumpet tooting "The Battle Hymn of the Republic" through his fist. Lloyd Seneca beat an inverted waste basket with an office stapler. Jack made paper airplanes which he hadn't done since high school, sailing them across the room, one majestic flight after another. The phone rang off the hook but no one answered. On the top of Jack's desk, Foxx was dancing to her own rhythms, champagne bottle in hand, so recklessly free of all inhibitions she became unrecognizable.

Meanwhile, in the gathering twilight, a bonfire was lit in the square. The high school band led hundreds of students marching into the area. Then the fife and drum corps began a snake dance and picked up a thousand more, all races and colors, men, women, kids.

At the *Sentinel* windows Jack saw his friend Frank climb the statue and spill a can of tar on the colonel's head. Then he heard a siren approach, not a police car but an ambulance. Not a sick occupant but a smiling Ruby Coles, together with Lukas and her two sons who had gone to fetch her, for all charges had been dropped. Jack saw her look up at the *Sentinel* windows as though she knew he was there. She raised her clasped hands over her head like a champion.

He hurried down to greet her.

"Thanks," she said.

That one word was worth the five million dollars.

Lukas shook his hand with head-shaking amazement. "You're one crazy motherfucker, J.C.!"

Jack took it as the ultimate compliment.

"You gonna win one for the fat man, J.C.?" Ruby asked.

"Opening day, Los Angeles, Ruby. You come, bring the kids. You too, Lukas. Box seats by the dugout. The works."

She nodded, overflowing with the way things were. He smiled at her, leaned over and kissed her.

"You're somethin', Ruby."

Suddenly, he was being lifted into the air by the gang from D.D.'s, demanding his presence at their own celebration. They carried him to the tavern where they sat him on the bar as if he were a barrel of ale. The sounds of "Black Jack!" chanting seemed louder than the roar of sixty thousand in a stadium. They were all there. Frank came to embrace him, eyes tearing in a wash of good feeling. Gus Guida was too loaded to get by all the bodies, but stood on a chair and waved—until he fell off. Dougie danced on a table top, pouring beer on himself. Someone started singing "For He's a Jolly Good Fellow" but never got past the first "fellow". The crowded air became as intoxicating as the booze. You could almost get drunk on the sounds.

For Jack, it drove home his victory. This was like nothing he had ever dreamed of. He had never been so in love with life, had never known what it was to feel so linked to them all. Nothing mattered but what was happening for everyone, and that made all the difference. In time, he stood on the bar, raised his hand to stop the bedlam. He was a sentimental drunk as he announced as fact that D.D.'s Tavern was the best place in all of Gandee—except maybe the offices of the *Sentinel*. He also raised a special toast to the new mayor. Great bursts of cheers followed. "D.D.! D.D.!" And D.D. raised his fist over his head as the celebration shifted gears to honor him.

Minutes later, it shifted again, this time to the astonishing cry of "Foxx! Foxx! Foxx! Foxx!"—the first time she had ever been welcomed by this crowd. In time she managed to catch Jack's eye, and drunk as he was, he could see that she had not come to celebrate. When he managed to get to her, she told him the news.

Jack's father had shot himself. Jack's mother had found him in his car, gun in hand, an empty bottle of whiskey on the seat, everything but a suicide note.

Foxx drove him home while he struggled to overcome his drunkenness. He wanted to be good to his mother. To be drunk at such a moment was to be insulting.

"Christ!" he muttered. "Christ!" trying to clear his head by repeating the name.

There were several cars parked out front. He walked to the front door and went in. No sound of grieving. Quite the contrary. There was a friendly chattering of ladies from the kitchen.

His mother saw his glazed eyes and went directly to the coffee pot.
He sipped slowly between deep breaths. There were others whom he
recognized as neighbors, but could not remember their names. He tried
to smile in greetings. He hated to seem stupid.

As for his mother, he could see that she was all right. She began to
speak, volunteering comment before he had a chance to say anything.
The big thing was that she wasn't really surprised. Jack's father was a
man who had had to have everything his way. He didn't know how else
to live. He couldn't deal with Jack's success. She told him how he'd put
on his Marine uniform on the day before the Black Jack Field opening,
stood in front of the mirror to feast on the sight of himself in all his
glory. Military heroism, that's what his life meant to him. Because of
the TV, he was even planning to wear it the night Jack arrived. Then
these last couple of days, she could see him breaking apart. He was
being punished, but he never for a minute thought he deserved it. He
could even feel sorry for himself. But when the *Sentinel* turned everything else upside down, John saw his life crumble like a house of cards,
so quickly, so all-of-a-sudden, he just gave up. He didn't know how he
was going to go on.

"Did he ever talk about Cyrus?" Jack asked. "Ever say anything?"

"Years ago, Christmas week, John and I came home and Cyrus was
sitting out front in his car. He wanted to know if you were coming
home. John told him no, you'd gone to Hawaii, I think it was. What
did he want anyway? Cyrus said you owed him some money. John told
him to leave, he didn't care how much or how little, he didn't believe
it anyway."

Jack half-laughed, half-sighed. "That was all?" he pressed it. "Dad
never said nothing after that?"

Whatever his father knew about Cyrus and him, it was buried
forever.

All this came tumbling out of her. In a way, his death seemed to
liberate her. She assured him she would be all right. Everything was
going to be fine, she insisted. He was so moved by this, for the first
time in his life he felt close to her. She took his huge hand in hers and
smiled. "With some things, it's never too late. I've always loved you,
Jack. I guess I was never strong enough to love you right."

For a while, they sat silently in Foxx's car. When she drove off he tried to note where they were going, then gave up, closing his eyes to let happen whatever would be. When she stopped, he sat up to see a cottage in the headlights. Her place, he assumed. She took his hand and led him inside. It was small and messy but comfortable.

"Do you want coffee, Jack?"

He shook his head, aware that she still held his hand. Almost before he knew what he was doing, he drew her to him.

It took a moment to gather the courage, not knowing how she might respond. When he felt no resistance, he kissed her. He was tentative, undemanding, his hands gently cupping her head as his mouth met hers. He felt her hands moving around his waist, fingers tenderly pressing his back. Encouraged, he drew her closer, holding her to him until he was overwhelmed by an emotion that took his breath away. He left her lips to hold his cheek warmly against hers. His arms went down over her shoulders as hers rose on his back, holding their bodies in a glorious mismatch. He could not believe the warmth of his feelings for her. He held her like one who wanted never to let go.

"Come to bed, Jack," she whispered.

He thought, if she hadn't said that, he might have held her there all night.

She took him to bed with silent sweetness. He could hardly believe that, too. Whatever tension he might have felt at this incredible tryst disappeared in the welcoming of her soft strong body. She was so completely pleased that he was there, he was enchanted by her, never before linking sex with such loving emotion. When they finally went to sleep, they were still locked in each other's arms.

In the morning, they made love again, thrilled by their new intimacy. After, he couldn't get over that such a night had happened at all. Too much had happened too quickly for him. He couldn't put it together with the rest of his life. He couldn't understand his feelings, only that the thought of going away and leaving her here seemed impossible to him. He began to ramble about her coming to California, how she had to get out of Gandee, how he could get her a job on a city newspaper. He could even picture it happening; there was nothing phony or far-fetched about it; Gordon could set it up with one phone call.

She said nothing, kissing his cheek the way you might thank your lover for bringing you a cup of coffee. She lay beside him, weaving fingers through his hair, leaving him to wonder what she was thinking. Then, suddenly, without a word, she left the bed for the bathroom and from there went directly to the kitchen, where she prepared breakfast. They ate poached eggs on toast, drank a pot of coffee during which she was pensive, busying herself with the serving and the eating until, at last, she said what was on her mind.

"I really don't think so, Jack."

He wasn't surprised. He could see that she had thought a lot about it.

"I was in New York once," she said. "With Fred Phillips." She pointed to a picture magnetized to the fridge. Her memories were obviously unpleasant, full of head-shaking, hand-waving, like one shooing a pesky fly. She told him of an intense young reporter from the *New York Times* researching a series of articles about the collapse of small towns. He'd come all the way to Gandee, mind you. He stayed for three weeks, picking her brains which she willingly allowed. She was so helpful, in fact, that he took her back to New York with an enticing promise of getting her a job on The Paper, as he called it—as if there were no others worth considering. His work was extremely well-received, largely because of her contributions. Fred never got her a job on The Paper but managed to get her pregnant instead. Noble fellow that he was, he'd given her a thousand dollars for an abortion then sent her back to Gandee.

She related this all lightly, as though it had no consequence one way or another, but Foxx could play such games to make herself seem less than she was.

"I'm no Fred," he insisted.

"God, no. He was an empty suit. You are a knight in armor."

"Then why do you keep that creep's picture?"

"To remind me how stupid I can be. Once you start forgetting what doesn't please you, you're just lying to yourself."

"I'll want a picture of you because it *does* please me."

"How will that sit with your woman?"

"I couldn't care less."

She smiled, "She probably wouldn't either."

She got up from the table, taking dishes to the sink. The thought of ending what had hardly begun seemed too heavy for him. He couldn't understand the depth of his feelings for her, only that he was hurting and couldn't handle the hurt.

"You could come, Foxx. L.A. ain't so terrible."

She appreciated his offer, but it wasn't right for her. Not at this time in her life. She explained about being an "outsider" again. She couldn't function in a big city. She wouldn't be able to accomplish what she could do here.

"You just set up a chance of a lifetime for me, Jack. You're leaving me with six thousand people. You saw what can happen if their newspaper sucks. Think of how good it can be if it doesn't. Jack, Jack, I'd be crazy to leave now. This is what I always wanted to do."

She saw him staring at her.

"What?" she asked.

"You're really beautiful," he said.

She left the sink to sit on his lap, then kissed him. He thought, the way she'd put down those dishes and come to him was the most endearing thing he'd ever seen. The kiss was a perfect ending to satisfy his soul. He was so full of her, he couldn't speak.

This was what it was to love someone, and knowing that became his triumph.

He had to go back to Los Angeles. They had both known that for several days. He made no mention of Judith, and Foxx did not ask him about her. He had commitments in Japan, and from there he thought he might go to the Philippine Islands to visit the factory where Black Jack athletic shoes were being made. Not a PR photo op but unannounced. More interesting that way. He would leave Foxx to run the *Sentinel* and be a part of the town reorganization. D.D. would have power of attorney over Jack's bequests as promised to the town and its electorate.

She drove him back to the hotel where he had to pack, arrange for his flight, call his mother, say goodbye to his staff at the paper. He did all these chores as she sat with him.

"We're like two ships that pass in the night," he said, remembering an old song.

She thought that wasn't quite right. "More like collided," she said, smiling through tears.

When they finally parted, words became useless, for everything that mattered was inside them.

Driving to the airport, he was fine until he saw the Shell station sign, a reminder of one last piece of unfinished business. This would be his last goodbye.

He left the Taurus at the pump for fuel as he walked around the service center, picturing the growth that he and Cyrus had cleared away, remembering that they'd even shoveled enough dirt to make a passable mound on which to set the slab. They'd painted the plywood home plate and cleared the setting, a ballplayer's island on a sea of weeds. But what he now saw was an insult to his memory. Not just an unused field but a garbage dump, trash scattered like wreckage after a hurricane. He defied the stench, kicked away old tires and oil cans and rusted parts of old cars, desperate to find that pitching slab. After eight years, what chance did he have? Could a two-by-four survive the weather? There was no sign of what might be left of the mound. He moved a tire, a chrome bumper, a rusted hood. He kept looking at the top of the Shell sign towering over the garage as a point of focus. He kept at it until there it was, the rotted slab in an overgrowth of weeds.

He got down on his knees to pull up clumps with his hands. He found a Coke bottle and scraped away stones and roots. In time, the two-by-four was liberated, and he stood behind it, looking to where home plate had to be. Then he toed the slab, leaned forward with his left hand behind his back, a pitcher looking to pick up his catcher's sign. He closed his eyes to re-create the validity of his memory and saw Cyrus again on his haunches, his heavy thighs pressuring his dirty overalls, the old black leather mitt targeted low over the plate, that high-pitched voice barking at him, "Look at the mitt! There ain't nothing in your life but that mitt!" It seemed so real to him, his body began to tremble with an onrush of emotion.

Tears came, as sudden as laughter, but he refused to move. He was crying for Cyrus and a lot more. He cried because it was his father who'd killed him and he was his father's son. He cried because all that had happened was connected to forces so vile he could not understand how such things could be. It no longer mattered that he'd beaten them, only that Cyrus was dead and the evil that had killed him was like a cancer in Jack's own soul. Had it not driven him to his own fucked-up conduct? Wouldn't it still be there like some unconquerable virus?

He had not really beaten them, had he? He had merely bought them off!

The thought was too heavy for him. It left him in limbo. He felt like a kid lost in a crowd with no idea which way to turn. He could count his blessings for they were endless, but something would always be missing.

"You don't even know that you don't know," Foxx had said. He had come to understand that. He now *knew* that he did not know, which of course frightened him all the more.

He found the eroded remnants of home plate then cleaned up the area to dignify Cyrus's domain. He took a five dollar bill and laid it on the remains of the plate as if it were a flower on his grave. He set a stone on it to secure it from the wind. "I'm sorry, Cyrus," he said, aware of the pathetic nature of his words.

He walked through the St. Louis airport amused at his memory of leaving it. He found a uniform official and asked where he might find Alvin. The man began to laugh at his answer seconds before he delivered it.

"Las Vegas, Mr. Cagle," spinning his finger around his temple in the age-old gesture of craziness. "Money makes the wheels go 'round."

"All or nothing, eh?" Jack said.

"That's Alvin."

"If he comes back, tell him I said hello and goodbye."

"He'll be back."

Jack moved off to the departure gate.

On the plane, he sat in a window seat aware of how tired he was. He stared at the action on the tarmac thinking of all that had happened since the last time. "Hortense Foxx," he spoke her name to brighten his mood. He had made his peace at leaving her after lovemaking, but when he got on the plane, the peace dissolved in a heart-stabbing loneliness fed by too much confusion.

He turned to see an old man take the seat beside him, small and wiry, horn-rimmed glasses prominent on his lean, lined face. The man nodded politely, indicating no sign of recognition. Jack nodded back, hoping that would be the end of it. He had no wish to talk to anyone.

He turned back to the window, watched the plane climb into a soupy cloud and then bank, and the whole world seemed to disappear. He shut his eyes and gave way to the memory of his last five dollar gesture to Cyrus, suddenly aware of how pathetic it was, embarrassing him as though others had seen and thought him stupid. It set off a chain of reactions, all of them disturbing. He had been through too much too quickly. He needed time to sort it all out, wanting to feel pride in what he had done, a sense of accomplishment that would have meaning for him. He wanted to revel in his victories and fit them into the texture of his new life. He had never thought of himself as complicated. His ups and downs had always been conditioned by simple problems. Anything that bothered him one day would seldom be around to bother him the next. But all that seemed different now. He was different. Everything was going to be different. Like what would Judith be to him, and he to Judith? Or Gordon? Or even Corky? How could he explain himself to them when he couldn't to himself? He had trouble making peace with these questions because he had no satisfying answers. He wondered about himself with an oncoming fear that he had become rootless.

"Champagne, sir?"

The flight attendant was lowering the tray in front of him. When he turned from the window to help, he heard the old man sighing, air hissing through his lips, and Jack saw the *Sporting News* brought close to his face. It surprised him, like seeing a pastor looking at a *Penthouse*. After all, this was America's national baseball journal. Not until the flight attendant laid snacks on their trays did Jack speak of it.

"You like baseball, sir?"

"Like it? Yeah, I like it."

"Something in that paper piss you off? I couldn't help notice."

"Oh, that. Yeah, something about one of them sports agents saying he didn't like the Series umping."

"You don't think much of agents, eh?"

"Never had one myself, but from what I can guess, they don't know enough to call a decent Little League game."

"You played ball, sir? Pro ball?"

"Before you were born, sonny."

"Did you go all the way?" Meaning the biggies, of course.

The old man smiled. "Had a cup of coffee." Meaning a brief stay at the top.

Jack offered his hand. "Cagle."

"Kutner. Mike Kutner."

"Outfielder?"

Kutner nodded. "Sixteen years in the minors, two more in the war, then one game in Chicago."

"Sixteen years for one game!" Jack was amazed.

Kutner saw the need to explain. "Ever been in love, sonny?"

The question rocked him. He really didn't know how to answer. "I dunno. I guess."

"There ain't no maybe, sonny. If you love a woman, you'd go half way 'round the world for one night with her."

Jack held back a smile, not to offend.

"You'd play for nothin', sonny."

"You mean when you were a kid, Mr. Kutner?"

"I mean it's a whole love story. That's what I mean."

"Nobody plays pro ball for nothin', Mr. Kutner."

"Name's Mike."

"Baseball is a job, Mike. Like everything else, you make a living at it."

"Yeah. Yeah. I got paid, sure, but that ain't why I played. Baseball was my life. My father was an immigrant, worked in the coal mines. He couldn't understand baseball, a game for kids, maybe. In high school, when I signed with Chicago for a couple of dimes, he threw my glove in the furnace! He was tryin' to stop me, like I was runnin' off with a dirty whore. I was gonna play pro ball, dammit! I was in love with it. When you're five-foot-five, 155 pounds, you sure better love it 'cause you ain't what they're lookin' for, not sayin' anything 'bout wearing these cheaters. Hey, I was good. Led the Southern Association in hitting, stolen bases, runs scored."

Jack was moved. He didn't hear talk like this. It *was* different now. Ballplayers played for money, and the size of their paychecks was the measure of their talents, and nobody ever said anything else.

"After all those years, how come only one game?" he asked.

"Oh, end of season stuff. Guys were hurt, they needed another outfielder just in case. I just sat in the dugout and waited. I knew I could hit these guys, same guys I'd hit for years in the minors. Then, the last game, they played me. It was like they say, terrible-wonderful."

"How'd you do?"

"Got a base hit, made some plays." Then he stopped, beaten by the end of the story. "I struck out in the ninth with the tying run on. That was the end, all right. It was like the woman you loved didn't want you around no more. If my father had been alive, he would've told me how I'd been crazy. All those years, wasted. Only my wife understood. 'You were in love,' she said."

Kutner was smiling, nodding his head. "Hey, it's all different now.

A lot of great ballplayers out there, like you, sonny. But too many third-raters gettin' paid millions. Big boys who can't hit their weight. Can't bunt. Can't run the bases right. Can't get wood on the ball. I hear them sayin' how they found God, you know, but by God, they can't find the cut-off man. They can't even stay in the batter's box, always half way down the foul line after every pitch, zippin' the velcro on their batting gloves, fussin' with their shirt, their caps, strokin' the barrel of the bat like it was their dick. All them look-at-me-TV superstitions. What *is* that? I was umpin' a high school game, some kid was doin' that, he kept poppin' up. I asked him why didn't he stand in there? He was never set. He looks at me like I'm nuts. 'Aint you *supposed* to?' he asks. Too much bullshit out there, all for show. Like tight pants to show your ass. Skin tight shirts. If a ballplayer wore a floppy shirt, then if a pitched ball just nicks it, it's an HB and he'd get on maybe a dozen times more. Base runners sliding head first. Don't nobody know you can *kick* a ball loose with your feet but you can't with your nose. Things like that, they add up.

"I'm sayin' it's sad. People say, it's the same all over. Politics, celebrities, zillionaires. But with baseball, it ain't right. If you love a woman, you don't try to get her to paint herself up like a store window mannequin. You want to love the best of her. For what she really is. You guys, you're like actors out there. Costumes and make-up, like you're givin' a damned show.

"I never stopped with baseball. I coached at the high school. Did some umpiring. Then I studied to become a barber, opened up a two-seater in town." He laughed at his thoughts. "I made more money cuttin' hair in a month than I made a whole season playin' ball. Called the shop 'Home Pate'. Photos of local ballplayers on the walls, Little League right on through. Kids come in to settle arguments about the rules. I ain't on the field but I'm still in the dugout, you get what I mean?

"Like now, I'm going to L.A. to see my grandson. Fifteen years old, damned good little second baseman, but my son-in-law is tryin' to discourage him. Too small, he tells him. Got my genes. Even looks like me, they say. I'm gonna tell him that if he loves the game, not to let anyone stop him from livin' the dream."

Jack took it all in. He looked at the old man, maybe eighty years old, whatever, older than anyone he knew. He saw the wispy gray hair, the leathery wrinkled face, the liver spots on his hands. But there was no doubt about the spunkiness that drove him. Because of baseball, the old man lived.

"Hey, didn't mean to buzz your ear, young fella."

Jack waved off the apology for none was needed. Pieces of his own life were blending in with the old man's words. Something had happened in Gandee, all right. And suddenly the fat black left-handed catcher behind the Shell station had become an old white man on a flight to L.A. "You gotta love it!" Cyrus had hollered at him, the cry that began it all. Jack looked at Kutner and marveled at the similarity of opposites.

Then, blessed by an insight that made more sense than anything Jack had ever experienced, he made his statement to the world.

"You still cut hair, Mike?"

"Did yesterday."

"How about cuttin' mine."

Kutner smiled. "Need shears, sonny."

Jack called the flight attendant.

"We need a pair of scissors, ma'm."

"Scissors? I'll see."

"And a comb," Mike added. "Couple towels, maybe."

In minutes, she was back with it all. Jack moved to the aisle seat, and Kutner draped the towels over his shoulder as he went to work.

"Cut it short, Mike," Jack said.

"No problem."

"Crew cut. Okay?"

And so it happened. Passengers stood by their seats to watch. The pilot made an announcement: "Flight 451 is proud to be witness to an historic event at thirty-two thousand feet, the shearing of Black Jack Cagle himself. Passengers are advised to remain in theirs seats as flight attendants pass out souvenir cuttings to all interested. Meanwhile, co-pilot Captain Everett Brady is offering his electric shaver for the removal of the celebrated Fu Manchu."

Jack smiled as the old man snipped away. And when the job was done, he had his crew cut, no moustache. The barber stepped back to admire his work.

"I'll tell you somethin', sonny: you ain't a bad-lookin' fella."

Someone came with a compact mirror and Jack took a long look.

"Hey, I remember this guy! A good kid, but all screwed up." He turned to Mike, grateful for it all. "What saved him, he really loved playin' ball."

Mike offered his hand and Jack took it warmly in his.

"Don't you forget that, sonny."

Eliot Asinof is renowned among baseball writers for *Eight Men Out*, his brilliant reconstruction of the infamous Black Sox scandal of the 1919 World Series. The author of five books of fiction and eight nonfiction books, he served an apprenticeship in the minor leagues as a prelude to his many works about baseball. His other novels are *Man on Spikes*, *The Bedfellow*, *The Name of the Game Is Murder*, *Say It Ain't So*, *Gordon Littlefield*, and *Strike Zone* (with Jim Bouton). His nonfiction books are *Seven Days to Sunday*, *People V Blutcher*, *Craig and Joan*, *The Fox Is Crazy Too*, *Bleeding Between the Lines*, *1919*, *America's Loss of Innocence*, and *The Ten Second Jailbreak* (with Warren Hinckle and William Turner).